"Now that's w
call flattering."

Gail dropped down beside Alec on the Persian-blue rug and added, "You really planned your color scheme for me?"

He reached for her, easing her down to lie on the soft pile. "Of course. I told the painters my woman has dark red hair and blue, blue eyes, and they took it from there."

She gazed up at him, her laughter dying away. His woman. Her man. "What makes you think I'm your woman?"

"This." He bent, taking her lips with exquisite gentleness. When Gail yielded to the delicious feeling, sudden heat flashed between them, jolting them both. Alec groaned and tightened his hold on her. "See?"

"Yes," she murmured, feeling the strong beat of his heart against her breasts, the heat and hardness of his body. "I *want* to be your woman . . . right now."

...ida native who was brought up on the same waterfront property where she now lives. After time off to raise two sons, she followed a career in newspaper writing until she and her husband, a commercial fisherman and watercolor artist, built a live-aboard boat and spent fifteen years fishing. Though they've since sold the boat, daily life for the McGaurans is still full, what with children, grandchildren and, for Joanna, writing. *A Simple "I Do"* is her second Harlequin Temptation, with more to come.

Books by Joanna Gilpin

HARLEQUIN TEMPTATION

163–FIRST MATES

Don't miss any of our special offers. Write to us at the following address for information on our newest releases.

Harlequin Reader Service
901 Fuhrmann Blvd., P.O. Box 1397, Buffalo, NY 14240
Canadian address: P.O. Box 603,
Fort Erie, Ont. L2A 5X3

A Simple "I Do"

JOANNA GILPIN

Harlequin Books

TORONTO • NEW YORK • LONDON
AMSTERDAM • PARIS • SYDNEY • HAMBURG
STOCKHOLM • ATHENS • TOKYO • MILAN

Published February 1989

ISBN 0-373-25339-7

A SILVER-GRAY VAN, polished to perfection and scrolled with fanciful violet letters that read *Coleman's Galleries of Art, King Street, St. Augustine, Florida*, pulled to a stop before a large, old-fashioned clapboard house on one of St. Augustine's ancient cobbled streets.

Inside the van, Gail Sheridan stole a look in the rearview mirror and thanked heaven for air conditioning. The late summer heat that had lingered into early September would have had her flushed and perspiring if she'd been in her own old car. Instead she looked cool, if a trifle pale. She pushed back an untidy lock of dark auburn hair, thought about lipstick and shrugged. Why bother? The day was over, and this was the street she lived on. She only had to deliver three framed prints, drive half a block south and she'd be home. Lena Coleman had said she could keep the van overnight.

Getting out of the van, she went around to open the rear door, then glanced at the three-story house. With its white picket fence and rambling roses bordering the path and climbing trellises of the cozy little entry porch it looked homey, full of storybook charm. No stranger, Gail thought absently, would ever guess that the door opened into a modern, well-outfitted doctor's office. Old Dr. Pennington had practiced in this house for years and brought up his family under the same roof. Now, according to what Gail had heard, Pennington had sold out to a New York doctor who intended to do the same thing.

Evidently another old-fashioned man, Gail thought, dragging carefully wrapped packages from the floor of the van, but a man with surprisingly good taste in modern art. Two of the prints he had chosen were beach scenes by Rolf Bleeker, excellent work and also expensive. The third print, done in brilliant primary colors and obviously meant for a child's room, was a life-size clown with a ridiculously cheerful grin, by L'Ebbe.

Peering around the light but large packages in her arms, Gail made her way to the little rose-covered porch and stood there a moment, breathing in the spicy scent of the flowers and listening to the hum of bees amid the creamy petals. The neat placard on the door informed her that Dr. Alec B. Morgan specilized in rheumatology and that his office hours were from 10 a.m. to 12 noon and from 2 p.m. to 5 p.m.

If she put the packages down, she supposed she could simply open the door, pick them up again and walk into the reception room, but it was after five o'clock, which she felt might mean that the house had assumed its role of home instead of office. After a moment's thought she rang the bell with her elbow. Footsteps approached, the door opened and Gail's eyes widened.

"Dr. Morgan?" she asked, incredulous.

"Yes?"

Swallowing, Gail stumbled on. "How—how do you do?" She had been watching this man lately among the early morning joggers on the bay front and the very last thing she would have expected him to be was an old-fashioned doctor. Or an old-fashioned anything. "I'm Gail Sheridan," she managed. "From the Coleman Galleries. Lena said . . . that is, Mrs. Coleman asked me . . . to bring you the prints you ordered." Regaining her composure, she smiled tightly. "If you'll just tell me where to put them."

The tanned face looking down at her eased into an answering smile. "Come in, please. I'll take that big one."

Gail stepped inside and loosened her grip on the largest package, allowing him to lift it away. "That's the clown," she said, quite unnecessarily, as the wrapping paper had split and one of the clown's bright eyes peered through gleefully. She frowned at the eye and set the other two prints down, leaning them against the reception desk. "I'll just give you your receipt, Dr. Morgan. It's here in my purse."

His eyes, she noticed, were a warm hazel with dark gold flecks that harmonized nicely with his tightly curled, close-cropped hair. He appeared to be in his mid to late thirties, and in the tailored gray slacks and white shirt he was wearing he looked quiet and dignified. She glanced away, remembering that in his jogging shorts he had looked entirely different, his nearly bare, muscular body bursting with virility and a tremendous magnetism. But of course she'd never made an effort to get acquainted. A man such as he was bound to be married, and besides, even after a year and a half of being a widow, she sometimes still thought of herself as Bob Sheridan's wife.

Now, keeping her eyes down, she went through her handbag and finally found the receipt. Since Morgan was still holding the big print with both hands, she laid the receipt on the blotter on top of the reception desk. She knew via the neighborhood grapevine that Penny Pennington, Dr. Pennington's spinster sister, had stayed on as receptionist for the new doctor. Penny would see that the receipt was duly noted and filed.

"There," she said, "everything in order and itemized. I hope you'll be happy with the prints, Doctor. If there's anything more the Galleries can do for you, just let us know."

"I know where I've seen you," he said suddenly. "You jog every morning along the seawall with a big Dobie. Is he a guard dog?"

Gail had always blushed easily and she did so now, surprised that he had noticed her in the morning crowd. Or had he simply noticed the Dobie, then her? Some joggers were wary of Dobermans, even on a leash.

"He's trained as a guard dog," she said, "but to me he's just a great companion. He's not at all dangerous under ordinary circumstances, if that's why you asked."

Morgan noticed the blush, watched her blue eyes slide away from his face. "Sorry. I wasn't criticizing. Actually, he's so well behaved I figured he had to be professionally trained." He smiled encouragingly as she looked back at him again. "He's a handsome dog, Miss—uh..." His eyes shot to her left hand and the slim gold band she'd never removed. "*Mrs.* Sheridan."

Gail smiled back, relaxing and moving toward the door. "Thanks. Well, then if there's nothing more..."

"Oh, but there is, I'm afraid. I told Mrs. Coleman I knew nothing about decorating, and she promised that when she brought the prints she'd help me decide where to hang them for the best effect. I expect you'd know, too, since you work for her. Would you mind taking a look?" He frowned slightly at her startled expression. "Of course, I know it's late—perhaps it would suit you better to come back tomorrow."

"No, it's all right," Gail said hurriedly. She didn't really work for Lena Coleman, except on Saturdays, but she was qualified to advise him on placing the prints. She had just finished a course in interior decorating and now rented her office space in the Galleries. She didn't bother to set Morgan straight. "If Lena— Mrs. Coleman, that is—promised help, I'll be glad to give it. Just show me the rooms you want them in."

He nodded, hefted the clown print and started off briskly. "Down this hall," he said over his shoulder, "then up the stairs. I've remodeled the living quarters."

Gail picked up the other prints and followed. The hall ran the length of the house, with doors opening off it into several examining rooms, darkened now but holding the sharp clean odor of antiseptic. The last door opened onto a flight of enclosed stairs, and she followed again as he started up. The stairs were steep, and turned abruptly toward the front of the house. The space was narrow, the walls dark, but halfway up was a high window that let in a ray of late-afternoon sunlight. At the top, there was an inconveniently small landing with a closed door. Watching Morgan carefully, Gail stopped midway, staying back as he balanced the big print on its side to open the door.

"While I was remodeling I should have rebuilt these stairs," Morgan said, glancing down at her. "As it is, I had to have some of the furniture lifted through the front windows." The touch of irritation in his voice faded as he studied her, his attention caught by the way the shaft of light from the window shone through her dark red hair, making a fiery glow that contrasted with the cool blue-green of her eyes. Her lightly tanned skin was firm, but there were fine lines at the corners of those remarkable eyes. So she wasn't as young as she had appeared at first glance. Pushing thirty, he supposed, though she had an odd air of naïveté about her, almost of innocence, as if nothing much had happened to her on the way from girl to woman. Not, he thought suddenly, that either her looks or airs were any of his business.

"Come on," he said abruptly, "I expect you'd like to get this over with."

She stepped up and walked through the door, looking around curiously. The remodeling had been extensive. Old houses were usually like rabbit warrens—lots of small rooms and dark halls—but this one was wide spaces and windows and golden light pouring in from the western sky. The whole front of the upper house had been cleared of inner walls and a modern kitchen had been installed on one side, with a dining table and chairs by the wide windows. On the other side of the large space were bookcases and an old brick fireplace, with a long sofa and big chairs upholstered in sand-colored tweed.

Surprised by the innovative changes, Gail silently let her eyes follow the walls upward, then laughed. "You did add a new dimension, Dr. Morgan."

He glanced at her and set the large print down, leaning it against a chair. "I like a lot of air around me," he said. "This is one way of getting it."

Overhead, half the third floor had been torn out so that the open space stretched up to the peaked roof, giving a feeling of immense height. The back half of the house, including both the second and third stories, was closed off from the open front by a long, newly paneled wall. A little stairway hugged the wall up to a small balcony and a door, which Gail supposed must open into an enclosed loft. Except for the bare walls and floor, the place looked finished. She put down the prints she carried and turned to him.

"There," she said, gesturing at the midpoint on the back wall, "is the spot for Bleeker's prints. The light from the west window will show them off, and if they're placed right, they're big enough and bright enough to dominate that long space."

Brows knit, Morgan stared at the wall as if imagining the prints there. "Yes," he said finally, "I think I like that. I'll get my tools. In the meantime, look around. The clown goes up in the loft, in my son's room. Of course, it's only a start. I need a lot of decorating advice, I'm afraid." He was gone, clattering back down the stairs.

Intrigued, Gail took him at his word. He had said to look around and he'd mentioned the loft, so she headed for it, going up the small open stairway to the balcony and opening the door. Stepping in, she felt a rush of warm approval. Any boy would love this big, airy room with its high, peaked ceiling and slanting walls, and the bank of windows to the east, looking out over rooftops to the blue shine of Mantanzas Bay. Lots of space for hobbies. There were twin beds, a dresser and a chest of drawers in heavy oak, but the room wasn't being used yet. The beds were bare, and an open closet was empty. Perhaps the family felt it would be more convenient to wait in New York until the house was ready.

"So this is where you are."

Gail turned to find Morgan standing in the doorway and watching her with a quizzical look on his dark face.

"I hope you don't mind, Doctor. After seeing what you've done with the living area I couldn't resist looking up here. This is a marvelous room for a growing boy."

Morgan relaxed and stepped inside. "I hope he'll like it. I want to have a desk and bookshelves built in on one side, and of course I'll need carpeting and curtains— something tough, I suppose." He gave the walls a sweeping glance, then turned back to Gail with a half grin. "I see I won't have to ask your advice about hanging the clown print. There by the door is the only space available. I completely forgot that the two long walls are slanted."

Gail laughed, thinking how openly he'd admitted his lack of forethought. A less confident man would have kept his mouth shut. "No matter. All you need is one good spot." She moved to leave the room, hesitating in order to give him time to step away from the door. She glanced up and caught him looking at her face with undisguised interest that faded so quickly she wasn't sure she'd seen it at all. He moved back as she passed him and looked away, a muscle tensing along the clean line of his jaw.

Then, following her down the stairs, he spoke gruffly. "I'm taking up too much of your time," he said. "Now that I know where everything goes, I expect I can handle the rest alone."

Gail stiffened slightly. He had wanted help, and with the expertise it would take to measure for the beach scenes, he needed it. But now he wanted her to leave. Why? Did he think she was too nosy, or was he bored? Actually, she thought, stepping from the stairs to the bare floor of the living area, she wasn't going to leave, whatever his reason was. It would be too tricky for one person to judge where the prints should hang because of the sharp shadow of the staircase on the left side of

the wall and the single door at the right, which, she
supposed, led into the master bedroom.

"We'll need a long measuring tape," she said, turning toward him as he came down the last few steps, "and
some chalk. Positioning two works of art to balance
each other on that wall is four times as hard as hanging
one."

He stopped, staring at her, but with the corners of his
wide mouth quirking up and his shadowed hazel eyes
obviously taking in the stubborn set of her jaw. After
a moment he nodded. "I suppose you're right. But it's
getting late. Sure your family won't mind waiting?"

"No family," Gail said, and began with the wrap-
pings on the two beach scenes. "No one waiting but the
dog, and my landlady will tide him over with scraps
from her dinner." She laughed. "She spoils him, and he
loves it."

Morgan was crouched over the open toolbox,
searching for the metal measuring tape and chalk. He
threw her a sharp glance and then straightened, the tape
and chalk in his hand. "I see," he said with a look of wry
understanding, "another one of the walking wounded.
How long have *you* been divorced?"

Color suffused Gail's face once again. She caught the
hint of sympathy, the fellow feeling of one human for
another when both have been through the same ordeal. So he'd been divorced and he thought she had,
too. People often did. No one connected a young
woman with widowhood. Still, it was a very personal
question he had asked, and hard to answer. "I lost my
husband over a year ago," she said finally, "and you're
right about the 'walking wounded.' Even after you're
on your feet, at times it's still painful. But it wasn't a divorce in my case. Bob drowned in a boating accident."

Shock flickered across Morgan's face. "I'm truly sorry," he said. "It was stupid of me to jump to a bitter conclusion. Please forget I asked."

"It's forgotten," Gail said quickly. "Let's hang these prints." She had the wrapping paper off, and now she broke the tension by carrying the brilliantly painted scenes over and propping them against the wall. "There. The colors look great against the paneling, don't they?"

"Yes. I like the effect very much." Morgan's gaze merely flicked across the prints before coming back to her face. His eyes were now warm and openly interested. "I'm going to need a rug. What color do you think I should buy?"

"Persian blue," Gail said without hesitation. "It'll pick up the deepest blue of Bleeker's oceans, and it'll go well with the furniture. Hand me that chalk and we'll get started on the measuring."

By the time they had measured, argued, remeasured and had the prints hung to their satisfaction, they were talking together easily. When Morgan carried the large clown print up to the loft, Gail followed with his toolbox, realizing how late it was only when they had to turn on lights to finish the job.

"I'm taking you to dinner," Morgan said, putting his tools back in the box. "It's the least I can do after all your help."

"That's not at all necessary, Doctor. All advice is part of the sale."

"Call me 'Alec', please. You've done a lot more than just advise me. Besides, I'd like your company. I'm beginning to hate eating alone."

Gail hesitated. "Thanks, but I'm not dressed for an evening out."

"You look lovely."

Gail looked down at herself. The aqua silk dress she had worn to work was neither fussy nor plain; it depended on its subtly flattering cut for style. It was becoming and suitable enough, but... "Thanks," she said again, knowing she'd like to go, yet uncertain. "But, well, I have to feed Puppy. He needs more than table scraps."

"*Puppy*? Is that what you call that huge beast?" Alec began to laugh. Taking her arm, he led her from the loft bedroom, switching off the light. "Isn't that a little misleading?"

"It's ridiculous," Gail admitted, smiling unwillingly, "but I started out calling him that while I thought of a good name, and then he wouldn't answer to anything else. Really, Alec, I should go home."

"If we do this right," Alec said, "everyone will benefit. We'll celebrate our artistic success over dinner—and bring Puppy two magnificent doggy bags."

All this time he'd been sweeping her along, down the stairs, turning on lights in the main room, turning on a light in the stairwell. His hold on her arm was warm and insistent as he guided her down to the first floor and outside to the backyard. When he opened the door of an old BMW for her, she gave up and got in, laughing a little, unsure of herself but seeing no graceful way to refuse. Puppy would be fine. He spent his days in a spacious, walled garden behind the house where she lived and Mrs. Langford fussed over him like a hen with one chick, bringing fresh water and tidbits. Actually, the dog had just been an excuse, and as Alec slid in the other side and started the car, Gail wondered why she had thought she needed one. She leaned back and smiled.

"Thank you," she said, "for talking me into this."

2

TURNING EAST on the dark, brick-paved alley that ran to the Avenida Menendez, Alec smiled. "I'm glad I managed to persuade you. I've been lonely here, and haven't had much time to meet anyone."

He glanced over at her, seeing her profile in the dim glow from the dashboard, her full lips curved in a half smile. His gaze dropped, skimming the shadowed shapes of her rounded breasts, the neat, taut waist and long, slender legs. A sudden warmth uncoiled and spread inside him, jolting him into a full awareness of how physically desirable she was. He tensed, then relaxed, telling himself it was time he got back to normal. "Truthfully," he went on, "I'm surprised you're free to go. I suspect you're usually dated up well in advance."

Her smile faded momentarily. Looking away as they turned onto the main street, she shook her head. "No, I'm really not. I have a lot of friends, good friends, but . . . no beaux." She smiled again, suddenly amused by her own old-fashioned word. "I was married for six years," she added. "I guess I still felt married for a long time after Bob died."

"It must have been tough to lose your husband like that," Alec said gently.

"It was bad at the time. We'd been friends all our lives and I missed him very much. But it's over—of course it's over. It has to be."

She looked away again, wondering why she'd felt compelled to say those words. They had left the Avenida, crossing the dark river on the Bridge of Lions, heading for the brilliant necklace of lights that was Anastasia Island, and she felt suddenly that she had crossed a different bridge inside herself. It *was* over. Bob was still part of her life, but a part that was now in the past. She turned back to Alec. "Where are we going?"

"Stover's Grill," he replied absently. "I think you'll like it." His strong, long-fingered hands clenched the steering wheel. "I was married for ten years," he said. "My wife divorced me eighteen months ago to marry a wealthier man."

She'd known he was divorced because of what he'd said earlier, but now she heard the deep bitterness he felt. He'd been hurt, and he was still hurting.

"I'd say that would be a big adjustment," she said quietly. "Changing your whole life. Making the move from New York to this small place. I expect it'll take some getting used to."

Alec shook his head. "It's not the move. I like small towns better than cities. But I can't get used to not having my son around. Bruce is nine, and we've always been close. Marian has custody now because of his schooling, but I'll have him during holidays and all summer. It's something to look forward to."

"So that's why you chose Dr. Pennington's place— so you could have him under the same roof with you, instead of stuck away in a house somewhere with a housekeeper. I wondered. Nine is a wonderful age, Alec. You'll have fun with him."

As they pulled into the parking lot of Stover's Grill, a small place famous for seafood and steaks, Alec's strong face softened. "He'll run me ragged, if you want the truth. But I'll love it. Come on, let's eat. Suddenly I'm starving."

Inside, an intimate atmosphere was created by low ceilings, deep booths and shaded lights and by the faint strains of music drifting through the air. Stover's did no advertising or offered any bargains; most of the diners who filled the booths were regulars who appreciated the gourmet quality of the food and the excellent wines. Alec ordered a mild Madeira as an aperitif and handed a menu to Gail.

Sipping the Madeira, Gail studied the menu and then, warmed by the company and the wine, laughed and handed it back.

"I can't choose. It all sounds delicious. Order for me, please." She honestly didn't care what she ate. A barrier inside her had fallen as they'd talked in the car, and the emotions she had held down for so long had escaped, fluttering like freed birds in her chest. Alec's vibrant presence made her feel fully alive and gloriously, carelessly happy.

"I do like a trusting woman," Alec said, raising his dark gold brows. "Maybe I'll order snails."

Gail winced. "I'll have a steak, rare, with salad."

He laughed and ordered the same, along with a carafe of wine. While they ate they talked, of everything and anything except the problems they had already covered in the car.

Later, over coffee he asked, "With a certificate in interior decorating, why are you working in someone else's shop?"

Gail laughed. "I'm lucky to have the space, and luckier to have Lena Coleman as a friend. I'm a very new interior decorator, just getting a start. So far my biggest job has been a guest cottage. Now you tell me how and where you grew up, and what you've done."

He gave her a sketchy account of what childhood was like in a small town in New York State. "I lived for sports until I entered college," he concluded. "By then I knew what I wanted, and premed leaves no time for play. But I don't regret any of the things I gave up or the years my schooling took. I like what I do."

"How did you happen to choose rheumatology?" Gail asked, because it seemed an odd choice for such a vital man. She would have guessed he'd choose a more dramatic specialty.

Alec frowned thoughtfully. "I saw too many people in pain and too little being done about it. My mother was one of them—suffering silently, passing off arthritis as just something that came along with age."

"Isn't it?"

Alec shrugged. "Not everyone who gets old gets arthritis. Not everyone who has arthritis is old. We need to find a lot of answers. In the meantime, the pain can be helped, the disease arrested, and a correct diagnosis can work wonders at times." He paused, then added gruffly, "I'll admit it isn't the best-paying specialty, but that doesn't really matter. My father left me all the money I'll ever need."

Gail looked up at him in surprise, thinking that was an odd thing to say, particularly on short acquaintance. "I see," she said, though she wasn't sure she did. "You mean you can do exactly what you want to and not worry about your future. That's wonderful, Alec."

"Yes, it is," he said, and dropped the subject. He had seen the look of surprise; he understood it and was angry with himself for mentioning his financial independence. It had sounded like the worst sort of bragging.

But Marian, his ex-wife, had nagged him so often to move into something better paid that he had gotten into the habit of defending his choice of medical specialty by pointing out why he didn't need the high income that came with high-risk surgery. He finished his coffee and looked up.

"Another cup? Dessert?"

Gail refused, smiling. "Just the doggy bags, please. If you'll come in when we get to my place and give them to Puppy, you'll have a friend for life."

Alec grinned. "Great. I'd rather have that Dobie for a friend than an enemy."

Driving back, Alec laughed when she told him she lived only half a block south of him. "Neighbors," he said, pleased. "How convenient, since I hope to see you again."

Gail merely smiled. She could have told him, if she'd wanted to, that the reason she'd asked him in to make friends with her dog was that she hoped he'd come back. Being met at the door by a fiercely growling Doberman had put off several persistent men in the past year, and she hadn't minded. This one, she would mind.

"Make it really convenient," she said. "Park you car behind your house, where you usually keep it. I'd better pick up the Coleman van and drive it home for the night."

A few minutes later, Alec had parked his car behind his house. He opened the car door for Gail and took her arm. "I'll guide you. The path around the house is dark and tricky. The roses along here have thorns."

"One of the ir-irrefutable facts of life," Gail murmured, and laughed at her own stutter. "Every rose has its thorns." She was slightly dizzy, and wondered if this was the effect of the wine or the company. Or both.

Then, as they started around the house, Alec put his arm around her waist and drew her closer. Tucked against his warm, muscular side, she decided it wasn't the wine.

"Sorry," Alec said after a moment, and drifted to a stop in the dark, scented air. "I find you ir-irresistible."

She started to laugh at his gentle mockery, but his hand cupped the back of her head and his lips covered hers. At first the kiss was light, but then he took her mouth with a sudden intensity, his tongue invading, his arms tightening.

Gail gave in to him, weak with the new sweetness of forgotten desire. Her body melted against his; her pulse raced; her thoughts whirled in a lovely, dark chaos. She was shaken as they drew apart, but so was Alec. He gripped her shoulders, staring at her pale oval face as if he didn't quite believe what had happened. Then he smiled wryly and let her go.

"I *am* sorry," he said. "I guess you really are ir-irresistible."

Gail managed a light laugh. "Don't apologize. It's not our fault. It's the wine and the scent of roses. Let's leave before we're victimized again."

His taut face relaxed into amusement. "Wait. As long as we have an excuse . . ." He was reaching for her, but she evaded his hand and went on, her soft laughter drifting back as she felt her way along the uneven path.

Catching up at the gate, Alec helped her into the van and got in himself. He lounged in the big bucket seat as she drove in the middle of the next block and parked in front of a large house. "The whole place has been made into apartments," she said, climbing out and heading for a hidden entrance on the north side. "I have half the downstairs, and my landlady lives in the other half."

Alec took her arm again as they followed the path to the entrance. She could feel his steady heartbeat against her, feel her own blood pulsing in her neck.

"I'll be quiet," he murmured in her ear. "The last thing anyone needs is an angry landlady."

"It's all right," Gail said shakily, pulling away as they reached the entry, "she's very tolerant of noise."

Alec watched her, head bent over her handbag. The tiny porch light turned her hair into dark fire as she searched for her key. "Sure it's all right if I come in?" he asked as she unlocked the door. "Will I get you in trouble with a boyfriend?"

Gail shook back her hair and looked at him, puzzled. "I told you—I haven't been dating. Some of my friends are men, but that's all they are, friends. No one has any claim on my time."

Following her in, Alec felt surprisingly strong relief, then a wave of caution. He had, of course, known that once he settled down and had time to meet people he'd be looking for the warmth and satisfaction of being with a compatible woman. But he didn't want to leap into an affair. Nor, he thought now, did he want to hurt someone who might be looking for more than he wanted to give. He waited, standing by the door, as she circled the small living room, turning on lamps. His gaze roved over the comfortable chairs and sofa, upholstered in a cheerful yellow print, the shelves loaded with books, the few but good paintings on the walls. There was a flourishing green here and there from potted plants, and a polished walnut glow from an antique secretary in a corner. Most of the lighting was soft, but there was a good reading lamp near one of the chairs. The mood of the room was serene and lighthearted. Like her.

"Sit down," Gail said. "Take the big chair, there. I'm going to let Puppy in, and it'll be better if you're sitting."

Alec didn't ask why. If the Doberman preferred a sitting guest, he was willing to sit. He leaned back in the deep chair, listening to Gail's footsteps receding toward the rear of the house and thinking how charming she had made the old, high-ceilinged room.

A quick scrabble of toenails on the bare floor of the hall was followed by a soft command. "Heel, Puppy."

Alec watched them come in, the slim woman and the large, muscular dog close behind her. He saw the dog tense as it spotted a stranger. Gail continued across the small room and sat in the chair opposite Alec. The dog followed and sat beside her, his long head up, his shining dark eyes hard and alert, fastened on Alec.

Alec grinned suddenly. "I feel as if I'm being inspected by a firing squad."

Gail laughed. "I suppose you are. He's even more protective in the house than he is in public. If you were standing, he'd stand between us and growl very rudely. But he just needs to know you're not a threat." She touched the dog and gestured toward Alec. "Friend, Puppy. Go shake hands."

The Dobie relaxed, his knotted muscles loosening into ripples as he padded over to Alec and sat, offering a paw.

Alec took the paw ceremoniously, then let it go in favor of scratching behind a sharp ear. Puppy relaxed further, his eyes half-closed with pleasure. Alec looked amused.

"That's all there is to it?"

"That's it," Gail said. "He won't forget. But those steak scraps won't hurt, either. Come on out to the kitchen."

Alec followed her down the hall into a cheerful room with a wooden table and chairs, delft-blue pottery on open shelves, white, ruffled curtains on a wide window and a rack of cookbooks over the refrigerator. Gail handed Alec the doggy bags and leaned against a counter, watching him sit on his heels to feed the scraps to the eager dog. She was surprised by his obvious pleasure in the task and by the way Puppy seemed to take to him. The Dobie accepted anyone on order, but he was usually reserved with other people. With Alec, he wagged his stump of a tail and pushed his long nose under Alec's hand to be petted when the food was gone.

"He likes you," she said as Alec rose and went to the sink to wash his hands. Alec laughed, slanting an ironic glance at her.

"He likes steak."

"Of course he does. But he usually takes food from a stranger with a very disdainful air. He likes *you*."

Drying his hands on a kitchen towel, Alec grinned, his hazel eyes warming. "Do you value his opinion?"

Gail smiled and turned away to open a cabinet. The sight of Alec Morgan moving around in her kitchen, his cap of tight bronze curls gleaming under the overhead light, the sheer size and power of his lean, purely masculine body and the way it dominated the small room, made her catch her breath. She felt as if she'd brought an exotic, possibly dangerous element into her calm, safe little world.

"Let's just say," she tossed over her shoulder, "that I find his approval reassuring, but not conclusive. I think I have a little brandy up here for a nightcap if you like."

He watched her stretch to reach the squat bottle on the top shelf, then moved behind her and took it down, brushing against her slender back. He was very close, and she was caught between him and the counter. She shifted to look up at him with startled eyes. Desire rose in him as he met her gaze, but he saw wariness there, deep in the blue, and he didn't want to push his luck. He handed her the bottle and moved away.

"Very little for me, Gail. Shall I get glasses?"

"Yes, please," she said faintly. "They're in the cabinet over the sink." When he'd brushed against her she'd felt his warmth and caught his scent—far more arousing than roses. His thoughts had been plain when she'd looked up. She'd seen the sensual softening of his mouth, the warm speculation in his hazel eyes. When he moved away she hadn't known whether she was glad or sorry.

Glad, she told herself as she poured the brandy. This was happening too fast, and her own senses, newly jolted into wakefulness, were too hungry to handle her attraction well. The kiss on the garden path had proved that. She handed Alec his glass and led the way back to the living room and the two chairs that sat facing each other.

"Very good brandy," he said easily. "Warm but not searing." He swirled the remainder in his glass and looked at her over the rim. "I've been doing some thinking about decorating my place, and I've decided the best thing to do is to hire someone with training to finish it. Of course I want you. If you're too busy now, I'll wait. I can live in the place as it is."

Gail sat up straight. "Just a minute, Alec. That isn't businesslike. There are things to consider...."

"Such as?"

"Why, how much you want done . . . your tastes and preferences. A—a budget. You'd be surprised what rugs and draperies and accessories can cost."

"That's not a problem. All I want is a place that's comfortable and livable and looks it. Nothing fancy. Nothing a nine year old boy has to tiptoe past." He leaned forward, put his glass down and gestured. "Look around. You've made this into a home. Just do the same for my place." He got up, stretched, then looked down at her with an engaging grin. "You can come over tomorrow and start measuring for draperies."

Gail smiled back at him, feeling a rising excitement despite her misgivings. This would be her first chance to take over someone's complete living quarters, correlate the styles, textures and colors and come up with a harmonious whole. "I'd like to try," she said somewhat breathlessly. "I'll do the measuring and planning, then make you a proposal. But I'm afraid I can't start tomorrow. Saturdays I help Lena Coleman in the shop. It's my busiest day."

"And I'm keeping you up," Alec said apologetically. "I'd better be going."

She walked with him to the door. "It was a very pleasant evening, Alec. Thank you."

"I'd like to be with you this weekend," he said, "but since you work Saturdays, how about saving Sunday for me?"

Gail hesitated, studying his expression. Then she smiled. "Sunday afternoon? I always spend Sunday mornings with my parents."

She had already told him her parents lived west of St. Augustine, across the San Sebastian River and some miles out into the country. He thought of saying they could drive there together. He hadn't seen much of St.

Augustine's surrounding countryside and it would be something to do. But perhaps he shouldn't make a point of meeting her parents.

"Sunday afternoon it is, then," he said. "I'll look forward to it. In the meantime I'll be watching for the dog walker at the crack of dawn." He saw the sudden, shy pleasure that flickered in her blue eyes and felt a small but definite leap of hope. Bending, he brushed her lips lightly with his, resisting a strong impulse to take her in his arms. "Good night, sweet. See you soon."

Gail watched him leave, noting the glint of his hair, the glimmer of his white shirt as he disappeared in darkness. Then she shut the door, letting out her breath in a soft laugh.

Picking up the brandy glasses, she went quickly down the hall to the kitchen, followed by the Dobie. The big dog went to the back door, where Gail let him out for a last time before he spent the night indoors. As she washed and dried the glasses and put them away, she thought of everything that had happened since she had stopped the van in front of the old Pennington house. In a way, it seemed to her that more had happened in those few hours than had happened in the past year and a half. She was alive again.

There was a scratch at the back door, a soft whine. Letting the Dobie back in, Gail bent and stroked him. "Promise you'll bite me if I start making a fool of myself?"

The dog leaned against her thigh, panting from his run outside. His sharp white teeth and red, lolling tongue made a striking grin against his gleaming black muzzle.

Gail tweaked his ear. "Stop laughing. After all, *you* gave him a character reference."

3

IN THE MORNING Gail was barely through with her fruit and coffee when Puppy laid his leash, warm and wet from his mouth, across her bare thigh below her shorts.

"Don't rush me," Gail said, but she got up and snapped the leash on his collar. She thought about seeing Alec in the crowd of joggers, and suddenly she was suffused with warmth. "We've plenty of time," she added breathlessly, going toward the door. "Can't you wait?"

Outside, the brilliant colors of sunrise were tinting the houses around them, and the fresh breeze from the ocean was beginning to flutter leaves on the tree branches overhanging the sidewalk. Gail tugged on the leash and set off at a half run. After a moment of surprise Puppy loped past her, pulling her along, muscles bunching beneath his shining black hide. Feeling foolish, Gail laughed and slowed, bringing the big dog under control.

"Sorry," she whispered, bending to run a hand along his sleek neck. "My fault, friend. The neighbors will think we're crazy, which you're not, but maybe I am."

By the time they reached the Avenida they were walking at their usual brisk pace, energetic but decorous. Crossing to the broad path along the seawall, Gail glanced around at the scattered walkers, runners and bicycle riders behind them. The slanting rays of the rising sun glinted on bronze curls far back in the crowd.

Alec passed her without slackening his speed, giving her a wide grin and tossing her a question. "Wait for me at the fort?"

Gail nodded, her breath caught in her throat, and watched until he disappeared among the other runners far ahead. He looked wonderful. A bronze gladiator. She walked only as far as the Bridge of Lions, then turned back toward the fort at the north end of the seawall. A massive structure of thick, coquina rock walls topped by black iron cannons, the ancient Castillo de San Marco was St. Augustine's main drawing card for tourists. The grounds around the moat of the fort were reached via a short flight of stone steps. There were benches set about on the grass, and when she reached one she sat on it, glancing at her watch.

She couldn't wait long, and maybe that was just as well. She was too aware of the deep warmth in her middle, the tingling skin and accelerted pulse that had all occurred instantly at the sight of Alec. Maybe the excitement was natural after a long time of denying her sexuality, but she had to settle down and put the attraction in its proper place. After all, Alec was virtually a stranger.

Gail was walking down the stone steps from the fort's grounds when Alec arrived. He stopped, blocking her way.

"Stay and talk a few minutes?" he asked winningly.

She smiled and shook her head. "Can't," she said with regret. "I have to leave now or be late for work."

The dog nosed Alec, and he bent to pet him while studying Gail's flushed face and her slim figure, clad in revealing knit shirt and shorts. "Would a few minutes late be so bad?"

She shrugged. "To me, it would. This is the day Lena needs me to be there. I'll see you tomorrow."

"After noon."

She smiled again, her eyes as open and blue as the sunlit sky. "Yes, after noon. See you then." She was gone, walking quickly away toward the alley that led to Charlotte Street.

Leaning against the stone side of the steps, Alec watched her go. She had exquisite legs, slender but delicately curved. He was a little taken by her leaving—what difference would ten or fifteen minutes make?—but what really had him off balance was that after only those few hours of being with her yesterday he couldn't get her off his mind. He had awakened this morning thinking of her.

Frowning, he straightened and left the grounds of the fort, heading for home. Was this what they called rebound? After his divorce several of his friends had cautioned him about getting involved too soon.

"When you're lonely you're vulnerable," one of them had said. "Take care, pal. You've been burned once. Next time look into premarital agreements."

Hell, Alec thought, staring down unseeingly at the old bricks of the alley. *I don't want another marriage, with or without agreements. Maybe I'd better back off a bit.*

LENA COLEMAN, middle-aged, plump, with a toss of blond hair above a round, smiling face, looked up from her desk behind the counter as the door to her shop opened. She glanced at the clock, laughed and went back to jotting down the week's sales.

"On the dot," she said. "As usual. If you're ever late I'll know you were mugged." She closed her ledger and stood, pulling down her tightly fitted, brightly colored overblouse and looking at Gail affectionately. "Tell me," she added slyly, "what did you think of the new doctor?"

Putting her handbag on a shelf behind the counter, Gail shot Lena a suspicious glance. "I thought he was very nice. Why?"

"Didn't you think he was handsome?"

"No," Gail said truthfully. Fascinating, yes. Exciting. Powerful. But handsome, no. To Gail handsome was a smooth, male-model face.

Lena sighed. "You're hard to please, Gail. I thought he was the best-looking man I'd seen since I married Hal. I also thought you two would make a lovely couple."

Gail shook back her heavy hair and leaned against the counter, eyeing Lena thoughtfully. "Is that why you suddenly couldn't deliver the prints or help him hang them?"

"Well," Lena said defensively, "I didn't think it would do you any harm to meet him. I mean, a youngish doctor, single and attractive . . ." Her voice trailed off as Gail cast her an amused glance.

"You," Gail said, "are almost as bad as my mother. However, I admit I liked him. He took me to Stover's for dinner last night and he's asked me out again tomorrow."

"Fast work," Lean said, delighted. "Now just hang on to him, for heaven's sake. Eligible bachelors don't come along every day."

Gail rolled her eyes heavenward and sighed. "We've just met, Lena. It may be a bit early to start planning what you'll wear to the wedding."

"He's interested," Lena began, "or he wouldn't have made another date—" She broke off as the door opened and a woman came in, carrying an unframed oil painting. Gail breathed a sigh of relief and went to help the customer. With any luck, the usual crowd would keep Lena too busy to advise her until closing time.

COMING HOME from a late shopping trip to the mainland that evening, Alec noticed the lights in the Galleries blink out as he waited at a red light just west of Lena Coleman's shop. Glancing at his watch, he saw it was nine o'clock. Just as he was about to drive on, Lena and Gail left the store. Lena walked west to her car. Gail slung the strap of her handbag over her shoulder and started east, but a man came out of a bookstore farther along and stopped her, talking a few moments under a streetlight. His manner seemed friendly and admiring, and Alec wondered if perhaps the man had waited for her and would take her home. But she walked on alone, so he waited until she crossed the street, then eased up beside her.

"Taxi, lady?"

Startled, Gail looked around. Then, as he reached to open the passenger door, she smiled and ran around to slide in, her face bright. "Oh, am I glad you saw me," she said, collapsing into the comfortable seat. "Usually I don't mind the walk home at all, but this has been a record day. Thanks for the lift."

"My pleasure," Alec said, very conscious of her warmth, breathing in her light floral scent.

"Aren't you taking a chance by walking home alone in the dark?"

Gail laughed. "This isn't New York, and it isn't really dark with all these lights. But I'm still glad to be riding. Nine to nine is a long day."

"It is. Want a drink before you go home?"

"Thanks, but no," she answered, smothering a yawn. "I'm afraid I'd be very boring company. All I can think of is bed."

Turning into the shadowed alley, Alec was silent. Gail was wearing a scoop-neck, lace-trimmed white blouse with her dark skirt, and the rounded tops of her breasts showed through the lace, gleaming ivory in the soft light from the dash. He glanced from those curves to the purity of her profile, the heavy mass of dark red hair, and an erotic vision sprang to his mind. He could see himself carrying her to his bed, tenderly removing her clothes, then slipping in beside her to take her in his arms. He could almost feel her softness, the warmth of her skin. Turning down Charlotte Street and approaching his house, he cleared his tight throat.

"Sure you won't have that drink?"

"I'm sure," she said drowsily. "It would be a waste. I'd just conk out." She sat up as they passed his house and drew to a stop at her place. Smoothing back her hair, she smiled at him. "I'll be back home tomorrow by one o'clock, Alec. Do you have any plans? How shall I dress?"

Her smile and the eager look that shone through her sleepiness were too much for him. He took her silky head in his palms and brought her lips to his. Gail sighed and opened her mouth to him, suddenly remembering and wanting his taste, his scent, the heated urgency of his tongue. The kiss was lingering and possessive, their mouths clinging.

Finally Gail forced herself to draw away, disoriented and breathless. "No more," she whispered, "please. We're going too fast, Alec." She opened the car door, her hand trembling, and slipped outside. "Good night, and thanks again."

Frowning, Alec drove back to his house in a tumbling torrent of desire both frustrating and puzzling to him. In one twenty-four-hour period he felt as if he'd given in to a crazy, supercharged magnetism that could only lead to trouble.

Going up the stairs, he told himself angrily that he'd made a bad mistake by getting involved with a woman like Gail, anyway. What he needed now was an experienced, worldly woman with a settled career of her own who could see the advantages of a quiet liaison with an established man. Someone attractive, but older and calmer. Someone sensual, yes, but a woman who'd been around enough not to expect any blathering about love. Now that he thought about it, he was sure Gail Sheridan would expect to find love in any sexual relationship. She was old enough, he thought, to have gotten over such illusions, but he was reasonably sure she hadn't. She would want to get married.

He made a Scotch and soda in a sparkling, never used kitchen and sat down in the darkened main room near the bank of wide windows, watching the stars while he drank. Tomorrow afternoon he'd pick her up and they'd find a nice place for lunch and talk, then he'd take her home and forget her. That would be best for them both.

GAIL SWORE an unladylike oath and turned the key again, for maybe the tenth time, frowning as she listened to the impotent grinding. Rousing the ten-year-old coupe that sat behind her house from Sunday to Sunday was always a chore, but the car was being particularly stubborn this morning. She got out, fuming, went to the cabinet on the back porch for her can of silicone spray. Marching back, she opened the hood to spray the coils and everything else she thought might have gathered moisture from the salt air.

From the back seat Puppy uttered the high, wavering whine he used to welcome a friend. Peering around the lifted hood, Gail saw a pair of tanned, muscular legs, every inch familiar, standing beside the car's back window. She straightened, pushing back freshly washed, flyaway hair and leaving a streak of grease on her forehead.

"Good morning," she said, conscious of her old jeans, her faded pink shirt, her hair blowing around her face. "We were just leaving—or trying to."

Alec stopped scratching behind Puppy's ears and grinned at her. "I heard and came to help. Sounds like your battery's getting discouraged."

He looked magnificent in those white shorts, she thought. He'd been for his run and his skin was gleaming like bronze. She wished she'd taken more pains with the way she looked, instead of dressing for the usual Sunday morning battle with the car. Feeling shy, she stepped out of the way as he came forward and peered at the old engine without much interest. "Don't worry about it," he added, "I'll drive you over. Just give me a few minutes to change and I'll be back with my car."

That was the last thing Gail wanted. Her mother was far worse than Lena; one look at Alec and she'd start hearing wedding bells. Virginia Winslow was a firm believer in both marriage and a frontal attack. She would probably ask Alec what his intentions were.

"It's nice of you to offer," Gail said stiffly, "but this one will start now. I think." She shut the hood with a decisive bang and got in, looking determined. The car started, coughed out a series of noises that sounded like a death rattle and stalled. She tried the starter again, but elicited only a faint buzz. She sat still, staring through the windshield, wordless and furious.

In the silence, Alec leaned down and looked in at her flushed face. "Go wash the grease off your forehead," he said gently. "I'll be right back."

Gail's hands tightened, white knuckled, on the steering wheel. "You won't like it, Alec. You'll be bored to tears."

"If you're there, I won't be bored." He touched her cheek, tilting her face to look into her eyes, remembering his decision of the night before. *Forget her.* He wondered who he was kidding. "I'd like to take you over, Gail. I like being with you."

She was mesmerized by the warmth of his gaze; her anger melted away. "That's very flattering," she said shakily. "How can I refuse?" At the moment she couldn't have refused him anything.

In the house Gail scrubbed her face, added lipstick, brushed her hair vigorously until it lay in its usual shining fall and changed her shirt to a crisp white one. Hearing Alec's car, she went out, locking her door.

"Where's Puppy?"

Gail stopped on the sidewalk. "I thought you might not like a dog in your car."

Alec grinned. "Puppy's a friend. Don't disappoint him." Watching her run back to get the Dobie, he thought of his son. Bruce had always wanted a dog, but pets of any kind were barred from Marian's exquisite

house. He got out, holding his seat forward as Gail
came back with the dog on a leash.

"Hop in, friend."

Puppy turned his long head and looked at Gail. She
gathered the leash in loops and placed it between his
waiting jaws. "It's all right," she said. "I'm going, too."

Motionless, the big dog watched her. Gail laughed,
went around the car and got in, shutting the door. With
a leap, Puppy shot past Alec into the back seat and sat
down.

"He likes to be sure," Gail said, still amused.

"I see that," Alec said, getting in and starting the car.
"He won't leave home without you. And I was just
thinking of stealing him for Bru."

"Bru?"

"Bruce, my son. Is Puppy safe around children?"

"He's safe around anyone who doesn't threaten me.
My husband was a professional animal trainer and he
taught Puppy to be a guard for me when he was out of
town."

Alec felt an unreasonable stab of jealousy. "He did a
good job," he said reluctantly, turning west on Cathedral Place. "It's hard to train a guard dog without
making him vicious."

"I suppose that's true. But Bob could do almost anything with a dog. He always could. He planned to be an
animal trainer when he was only a child. I remember
when I was eight and he was ten I helped him put on a
neighborhood circus." Gail leaned back and laughed.
"I was a clown, and he had a wild animal act. He had
taught his dog an amazing number of tricks, even
jumping through hoops."

Glancing over at her, Alec saw nothing but an
amused memory lighting her eyes. "So," he said, turn-

ing into the westbound lane of King Street, "you married the boy next door."

"Literally," Gail acknowledged, still looking reminiscent. "The families were very close and I guess I was Bob's other plan for the future. Neither of us ever had a real date with anyone else, and once Bob had his business established we were married." She smiled. "In a way it was like marrying a member of the family, we all knew each other so well."

That explained her air of naïveté, Alec thought, her look of innocence. Nothing much *had* happened to her on the way from girl to woman.

"Tell me about your parents," he said, and leaned back, relaxing into the seat as he drove. The day was perfect; one of those few September days in Florida that feel like fall, and the traffic on Sunday morning was light. He glanced over at Gail, thinking how fresh she looked, what a clear, deep blue her eyes were. "Do you resemble your mother?"

"A little, I think. But my father is the redhead. Or was. He's older than Mom and he's silver haired now. They're . . . well, they're the usual parents. Dad's retired and spends most of his time in his woodworking shop. Mom spends her time worrying about me. I get a lecture every Sunday morning on settling down."

Alec laughed. "Does she see you as a swinging single?"

"She sees me," Gail said wryly, "as a lonely widow, blindly ignoring a whole world full of marriageable men. Don't be surprised if she gives you some heavy hints on what a good wife I would be."

Alec waited a moment before responding. "That seems normal for most mothers, I guess. What have you got against marriage?"

Gail flushed. "Is that how I sounded? I'm not putting marriage down. It's just that, well, I'm on my own for the first time and I find I rather like it." She glanced over at him and laughed a little. "That's what Mom doesn't understand. She went from her father's house to her husband's house and she's never been out on her own. Or wanted to be."

"But you do?"

"Yes," Gail said firmly. "I was just like Mom, always someone's dependent, and when Bob drowned I was absolutely lost. Now I want to be able to count on myself. I guess to do that you have to learn to make your own decisions and run your own life. So that's what I'm going to do."

"I'd say you're doing very well," Alec said, smiling. "But I'd also say you'll probably make a very good wife when you get around to marrying again."

Gail stared at his strong profile. "That's really a snap judgment," she said finally. "You'd have to know me a lot longer than a couple of days even to make a guess on that."

He shrugged. "Time is relative, remember. I've known some women for years without finding out what they were like. On the other hand, you're right up front with what you think and feel."

Gail laughed. "I'm an open book? That's terrible, Alec. I've always heard women are supposed to be mysterious." They were crossing a short bridge, and she gestured to the right. "Head north, but take the island lane and turn left at the third traffic light. After about ten or twelve miles, brace yourself for Mom."

He switched lanes easily in the light traffic, then glanced over at her, amused. "The prospect doesn't bother me," he said. Which was true. He felt good—relaxed and happy, looking forward to the day. There was nothing to worry about; Gail didn't want marriage, either.

4

THEY DROVE through several miles of congested suburbia, coming at last to a section with large lots and homes set back from the road. In the back seat, Puppy sat erect and whined. Gail turned around and rubbed the dog's forehead soothingly.

"He knows we're nearly there," she said. "He loves the place. Lots of room to run and no leash law." She unsnapped the leash and coiled it, putting it in her bag before facing forward again. "Third driveway on the right when you pass that big oak, Alec."

He nodded. "Got it." He could tell that the dog and Gail were both looking forward to the visit. In spite of her amused criticism of her mother, he decided, Gail must enjoy her family. He liked that. Swinging into the driveway, he saw the front door open. A slender woman with a streak of white in her dark hair came quickly down the steps.

"Gail! Darling, you're late! We were afraid you weren't coming, but here you are. And with company, too. That's marvelous! Your father is in the kitchen, peeling apples. Do let Puppy out before he breaks a window...."

"My mother," Gail said, looking at Alec with a grimace, "and in fine form. Mom, this is Alec Morgan."

"How do you do, Alec." Virginia Winslow wrestled the car door open, then stood and laughed as Puppy galloped past her, heading for the trees behind the house. "Just look at him go, bounding like a hare." She turned back to them, her green eyes sparkling, and looked up at Alec as he came around the car to help Gail out. "My," she added, suddenly interested, "you're a big one, aren't you? How long have you know my little girl?"

"Not nearly long enough to suit me," Alec said, grinning at the suddenly pained expression on Gail's face. "But I'm working on it."

"Wonderful," Virginia said, hooking an arm through his and reaching for Gail's hand. "You'll never regret it, Alec. She's a lovely person, if I do say so myself. Come in and meet her father. By the way, what do you do for a living?"

"Mother!"

Virginia laughed gaily. "Gail thinks I'm bold," she confided to Alec. "But if she doesn't tell me about her friends, what can she expect? Naturally I'm interested."

"I see that," Alec said, enjoying himself enormously. He looked past Virginia at Gail, who was caught between anger and laughter. "You should communicate with your mother, Gail. Why haven't you told her about me?"

"Because," Gail said, "the last time I saw her I didn't know you."

"How romantic, darling!" Leading them both firmly toward the house, Virginia beamed. "You've only just met, and you're already bringing him to meet us. You've never done *that* before. Maybe it's a sign."

"My car wouldn't start, Mother. Dr. Morgan was nice enough to offer me a lift."

"A *doctor*? Really, Gail? How nice!" Sweeping them into the house, Virginia forged through the living room and into the kitchen, her slender hands still grasping them both. "David, do put down that knife and greet our guest...."

Hanging back, Gail glanced at Alec and caught such a look of rich amusement that she had to laugh. Her embarrassment melted away. She smiled as she offered her cheek to her father and hugged him. A tall, calm and pleasant man, David Winslow kissed his daughter, shook hands with Alec and then took off the apron he was wearing.

"There's enough apples for two pies, dear," he said to his wife. "Anything else I can do?"

"You can amuse Dr. Morgan while Gail and I finish the pies," Virginia said promptly. "I want to talk to her."

Gail groaned, her father laughed, and Puppy rattled the back door with a short, sharp bark. Virginia rushed to let him in.

"Hello, gorgeous," she crooned, bending to pet him. "Did you have a good run? Wait until you see the bone I have for you."

The Dobie leaned against her, enjoying the attention, and Gail looked at Alec.

"I'm sorry," she murmured helplessly.

"I'm not," he murmured back. "Haven't you ever heard that Mother knows best? She thinks I'm wonderful."

"You're as bad as she is," Gail retorted, trying not to laugh. She raised her voice as her father came back from hanging up the apron. "Take Alec to your shop, Dad, and show him the chest you're making for me. I'm sure he'll be fascinated."

Getting out the sugar and spices while Virginia mixed the crust, Gail waited until the two men had disappeared in the direction of her father's woodworking shop before speaking quickly and decisively.

"No matchmaking, Mom. I mean it."

Her mother laughed, her face lighting up. "It's plain he's got his eye on you. I can tell."

"Rebound," Gail said flatly. "He's been through a bitter divorce and he's still hurting. Leave him alone."

"Don't be silly. That's one of the best times to catch a man. You'd be crazy not to grab him, Gail. He's educated and intelligent, and so darn good-looking! How can you resist?"

"Good Lord," Gail said, disgusted, "I *told* you. We just met! One more leading remark from you, and I swear I'll leave."

Virginia finished patting the pastry into four balls, then began to roll them into neat circles. "All right, darling. I'll be careful." She turned back to meet Gail's eyes. "But any man would be lucky to get you, especially after a bad experience with another woman. You know how to love a man—I saw that with you and Bob. You made him so happy."

Gail looked away. "That was different," she said after a moment. "Bob and I grew up together. I knew what he wanted."

"That's the whole point," Virginia said, suddenly serious. "You didn't just know, you gave. Some women only take. That's why I said this man would be lucky if—"

"Shh. They're coming back." Gail turned and faced her mother again. "Mom, *please*?"

"All right, I promise." Virginia put an arm around Gail's waist and gave her a quick squeeze. "Mom will be mum."

The morning went quickly. The men talked sports, argued baseball teams and got along famously. Gail found a ball and spent a half hour throwing it for Puppy on the back lawn, then came in to help Virginia with the rest of the huge dinner she always served on Sunday.

"Somehow," Virginia said wistfully, "this feels like a family. Or would, if there were a few children around."

"Now, Mom," Gail warned, and her mother glanced at the open door.

"He can't hear me out there," she said. "Don't be so picky. Anyway, he couldn't blame me for wanting a grandchild or two. That's one thing I really regret—that you had no children with Bob. I know, it was Bob's idea to wait, not yours. I just wish you'd overruled him."

Gail started to say that would have been wrong, that a baby deserved two parents who wanted him, but Alec spoke behind them.

"Dave sent me after a couple of beers," he said genially. "Hope I'm not getting in your way."

"Not a bit," Virginia said quickly. "I'll get them for you." She opened the refrigerator and began searching.

Behind Virginia's back, Alec met Gail's eyes with such warmth in his gaze that her knees became weak. He had looked strange in her kitchen, but here he seemed to be at home, part of the family and perfectly at ease, giving his woman a secret promise for later. Gail could feel heat climbing her neck and cheeks. She turned back to stirring the rich beef gravy her mother made, her slim fingers trembling on the wooden spoon.

"Here you are," Virginia said gaily, straightening and handing Alec two glistening cold bottles. "Tell David it's all you'll have time for. Dinner is almost ready."

"He won't mind that," Alec said, smiling down at her. "The smell of that roast is making our bellies growl."

Gail pretended to be engrossed in the gravy and refused to look around as he left. She heard her mother sigh.

"What belly?" Virginia asked in a low tone. "He's as flat as a pancake. What a gorgeous physique he has. How *can* you resist him, Gail?"

Gail turned her head stiffly. "Looks aren't everything, Mom. I need to know what a man is like inside."

"Oh, of course. But he seems mighty nice to me. Let's finish this before they decide we're trying to starve them."

"HOW LUCKY YOU ARE," Alec said on the way home, "to have parents like that. They're a wonderful couple."

"I know." She was on her knees, leaning over the back of the seat and snapping the leash on Puppy's collar. Finished, she turned around, giving Alec a small smile. "Once my mother stops trying to push me into the nearest male arms, I enjoy my parents very much."

Alec laughed, then sobered. "It's natural, Gail. She's of the generation that believed all women should be married. Don't be too hard on her. She only wants you to be happy."

Gail sighed. "You're right, of course. But I *am* happy. I like my life. In fact, I'd need to think very seriously before I entered into any kind of new relationship."

Alec settled back, his wide mouth curving into a faint smile. "What's on your list?"

"My list?"

"Your requirements for candidates."

Gail glanced at him and laughed. "I'm afraid I'm not all that scientific. Suppose I found a man who fulfilled all the requirements and left me cold? I'd feel foolish."

"Then you have no requirements?"

"I didn't mean that exactly," Gail said thoughtfully, "I guess I'd require love, and trust. But those two things you can't ask for. Either they're there or they aren't."

Love. The standard illusion. And *trust*? Alec winced inwardly, turning onto the highway and starting south. She sounded incredibly naive. But, then, she hadn't learned the hard lessons he had about what could happen to illusions. He drove faster, suppressing a sudden wish to tell her she'd be happier if she stuck to realities.

"Some list," he said finally. "Aren't you a little concerned about other things?"

"Other things tend to work out," Gail said carefully, "if the feelings are right." She was uncomfortable. She felt his tension, but she didn't understand it. "Let's talk about something less serious. What would you like to do this afternoon?"

They had turned east across the bridge into old St. Augustine and right in front of them was a large sign advertising all the various tourist attractions. Alec glanced over at her and laughed.

"How about hiring a horse and buggy for the grand tour? I've been here almost two months and I've never even seen the inside of the fort. You can be my tour guide."

Gail broke into laughter. "Wonderful. Even though I'm a native it'll be my first tour, too. Let's take Puppy home and leave your car at your house. I need the walk to the fort after my mother's dinner."

An hour later, leaning on the parapet of the fort with the sea breeze ruffling her hair, Gail intoned, "'The walls of Castillo de San Marcos are sixteen feet thick at the bottom, tapering to seven feet at the top, and are built of coquina rock put together with oyster shell and mortar. Construction was begun in 1672 by Spanish soldiers and finished around 1702.'"

Alec laughed and draped an arm around her slim shoulders to pull her close. "You take your tour guide duties seriously, don't you?"

"Certainly, sir." Pretending pride, Gail rested a proprietary hand on one of the huge black cannons that nosed through the wall. "This is a national monument, sir, and one of the few invulnerable forts ever built. Not even the Americans could take it."

Alec gently kissed her temple. "Then how did we get it?"

"Not by force," she answered, "by treaty." She heard the tremor in her voice and turned to look out over the inlet, too conscious of his warmth against her, the strength of his arm as it held her. She could be friendly and casual as long as they stayed a few feet apart, but when they touched she couldn't think, only feel. She tried to ease away, but he held her firmly.

"Are you invulnerable, Gail?" he asked softly. "Will I need a treaty before you allow me inside your walls?"

She turned her head and looked into his shadowed eyes, inches from her own, and knew he could storm her walls without a shot being fired. Her defenses were crumbling like sand, swept away by the tide of her own desire. She reached up and touched his hair and was surprised by its softness. "Do you intend to be my enemy," she asked in a whisper, "or my friend?"

Alec could see surrender in her darkening blue gaze, in the soft parting of her lips, feel it in the gentleness of the fingertips that touched his hair. He was jolted by a surge of triumphant passion, mixed with a sudden pang of tenderness he didn't understand.

"Neither," he said huskily, "I want to be your lover." Oblivious to the strolling sightseers behind them, he kissed her parted lips hungrily, pressing her slim body hard against his own. Gail responded with a gasp, her fingers tightening in his hair, her body yielding to his. Then, as she heard a subdued remark and a low laugh from a passing couple, she pulled away, her face red.

"We're acting like teenagers," she whispered.

Alec leaned against the wall again, breathing hard. "I don't care. I feel like one. I'm crazy for you, Gail."

She shook her head and moved away a little, turning to look out over the peaceful Sunday scene below. "Let's go and finish the tour," she said after a moment. "It's safer."

They took the first of the gaily painted open surreys lined up at the seawall, acquiring an ancient driver and an equally ancient horse, and went through the restoration area, then plodded across town. At Zorayda Castle, a miniature replica of a wing of the Alhambra in Spain, they wandered through the galleries, looking at threadbare Oriental rugs, pierced brass jugs and intricately carved furniture. Upstairs, Gail peered through the artfully constructed window of the seraglio, built to allow the women of the harem to see out without being seen, then backed away and sneezed.

"Get me out of here," she said, laughing. "I can't see through the glass for the dust. It must be antique dust, too valuable to wipe off."

"They brought it from Spain, no doubt. Come on, I'm all toured out." Alec took her arm as they went down the worn stairs and back out to the surrey.

When they were underway again, Alec glanced at Gail, who sat calmly on the old leather seat, her hands folded in her lap. Leaning back, he reached for one of her hands and entwined his fingers with hers. Their joined hands rested on her thigh.

"It's nearly five o'clock, sweet. We'll stop at my house for a drink and decide where we'll spend the evening."

Gail smiled slowly, leaning back on the cracked leather and watching the tattered, multicolored fringe on the top of the surrey sway with the uneven gait of the old horse. She had decided before they left the fort that she wouldn't be alone with Alec this evening, but with the driver only an arm's length away, she didn't risk an argument. Time enough to tell Alec on the walk home.

Standing at his gate an hour later, she told him. Leaning against a post, Alec looked down at her in the growing twilight and frowned.

"Why?"

"We've been together every spare minute since we met," Gail began. "And . . ."

"You're tired of my company?"

"No. You know better. I've enjoyed it all. But I . . . have things to do. Like laundry. I work all week, you know, and I—" She stopped, her brilliant eyes clouded, searching his face. "I guess you know I'm making excuses, don't you?"

"Care to tell me the truth?"

"I'm scared," Gail said simply. "I have some feelings about you I can't handle. Laugh if you want to, but I need some time alone, so I can think. Good night, Alec."

He caught her arm as she turned and swung her back. "I'm not laughing," he said huskily. "I'm having trouble myself. I know I've been rushing you, but I can't seem to stay away. I've never wanted anything in my life as much as I want you." He hadn't meant to say that much; the words had spilled out before he could stop them. He swallowed, staring at her. She was becoming too important to him. Something about her had reached past the careful barriers he had built, and suddenly he didn't like it. He loosened his grip on her arm and straightened. "I'm sorry, Gail. Maybe we both need to think. When should we meet again?"

Gail's lips softened into a smile. "If you still want to see me, I'm free Saturday at nine."

"You're going to think for a *week*?"

"You are, too," Gail said softly. "Maybe you'll find out that you feel the way you do about me only because you're...just missing someone. Maybe we'll both settle down and get to know each other before we get involved. Let me go, Alec."

He watched her walk briskly across the street and down the other block to her house, then he turned and went into his, the scent of the roses along his path reminding him of the first time he had kissed her. "I'm scared," she had said, and so was he. Scared to death he was going to lose her. If these feelings were what his friends meant when they talked about rebound, they'd been right to warn him.

ALEC WENT BACK to his solitary habits, watching for her auburn hair glinting in the distance at dawn. He was puzzled and half-angry with her, but determined not to show it.

They talked occasionally. Meeting in the early light, avoiding each other's eyes, they would pause for a moment along the seawall. Giving Puppy a pat or two,

Alec would mention the weather; Gail would ask polite questions about his remodeling, and contragulate him on his growing practice. Then they would nod and smile and go on. On Wednesday they met by accident on the steps leading up to the grounds of the fort; there was no one around them. Stepping aside to let Gail pass, Alec couldn't resist asking one question.

"Tell me," he said, "what kind of thoughts are you having this week?"

Gail looked away. "Confused. But productive."

"Productive of what?"

"Decisions."

Staring at the rounded line of her cheek, the firmness of her chin, Alec saw no indication of what her decisions might be. He was suddenly afraid to ask. "I suppose," he muttered, "that's the whole point of thinking." He went on, breaking into a lope when he reached the bottom of the steps.

Gail went home, carrying with her the fear that she might have lost the love of her life by being so cowardly and pushing him away. There hadn't been an hour when she didn't wish she could see him, but still she knew the week apart was a good idea. She'd worked through the questions she had about her own feelings. It was not a case of purely physical desire—though that was certainly there. It was not a case of loneliness, either. It was Alec. Puzzling, ironic, somehow bitter Alec, who could turn her heart over with one of those *I want you* glances.

Yet wasn't there always a hint of doubt mixed in with his desire? She frowned. He had said he wanted her more than he had ever wanted anyone before. But he still seemed to be holding something back, perhaps for the same reason he was ironic and bitter.

Going into her house, Gail felt a catch in her throat, a presentiment of danger. She was teetering on the edge of falling in love with a man she didn't understand. Maybe it would be best if he decided not to see her again.

Saturday morning Gail took Puppy on a new walk. West on Cuna, south on St. George to Cathedral Place, then back the same way, avoiding the seawall, and a meeting with Alec. She was afraid he might simply pass her with a casual greeting and a look of indifference, neither of which she thought she could bear.

"Either he'll call or he won't," she said, unsnapping Puppy's leash. "By this evening, we'll know."

The Dobie yawned, exposing long, razor-sharp teeth. Gail laughed shakily. "I'm boring you? Sorry, friend."

But who else could she talk to? Dressing for work, she cringed at the thought of talking to Lena or, worse yet, her mother. She needed an ear, not a mouth. Especially not a mouth that would tell her how wrong she was to rudely put off such a highly eligible man.

By six o'clock Gail was sure Alec wouldn't call. The phone at the shop had been ringing all day, and every ring had lifted her hopes, then let them drop with a thud when she answered. But the flood of orders had at least brightened Lena's face.

"I would guess," Lena said later during a lull in the evening, "that you have a date tonight with that good-looking doctor. You're dressed for it. I love that blouse on you, by the way."

Gail looked down at the scoop neck and frowned.

"Guess again," she said unevenly. "I'm going home."

"Oh?" Lena looked sympathetic, then shrugged. "He'll be back. A man likes to play the field in a strange town."

Silent, Gail started rehanging some prints. She could think of a half-dozen attractive women who were on the lookout for a man. Any man. She laughed suddenly. "Scratch one," she said. "I'm not an entry in any field! That sounds like a horse race."

Locking the door at nine, Lena asked, as she always did, if Gail wanted a ride home. "It smells like rain," Lena said, sniffing the cool wind. "You may get wet."

Gail waved farewell. "I'll walk. I need it. But thanks, anyway." She turned away as Lena left, and started off. She did need the walk tonight. She needed to get her emotions under control. She'd been thinking like a child. She looked ahead and relaxed, seeing Tom Swenson locking up his bookstore. He waited every evening to speak to her, to tell her some whimsical joke he'd heard and to offer her a ride home. They'd known each other all their lives and had always been friends. Gail felt better than she had all day as she came up to him.

"Wait until you hear this one," Tom said, his lean face wreached in a grin. "It's really funny."

Gail stopped. "I can use a good joke, Tom. Tell me—" She broke off, glancing up as a patter of heavy rain caught them. "Oh, damn," she added, dodging under an awning. "It's going to pour. I can use a ride home, too."

Across the street, Alec watched as the man from the bookstore grabbed Gail's arm and dashed with her to a small station wagon parked half a block away. They were both laughing, scrambling into the car. It had been the threat of rain that had given Alec an excuse to pick up Gail. Now, his face grim with disappointment, he drove home.

He parked his car behind his house and sat a moment, struggling with his feelings. Of course Gail had other friends; this didn't necessarily mean she had decided she was through with him. He'd call tomorrow. Leaving the car, he fumbled for his keys and found the key to the back door missing. Par for the course. It was pouring rain and he'd have to walk around . . . no, he wouldn't. Getting back into his car again, he drove around and stopped in front, noticing as he did that the station wagon was parked in front of Gail's house. He tried to rationalize the pain twisting his belly. Certainly it wasn't jealousy. Or was it?

Peering through the streaming windshield, Alec saw the man from the bookstore come out again and dash for his car. He waved back at Gail as she stood in her doorway, and drove away.

Alec grinned, feeling the pain in his belly miraculously disappear. It was raining; naturally the man would offer her a ride home and see her inside. He thought of going into his house and calling her, but instead he started his car and drove over to her house. If she had decided not to see him again, he'd hear it in person, not over the phone. He parked the car, looking at the glow of light from her windows. As he fumbled with the door handle, he noticed with surprise that his hand was shaking.

Gail, having taken off her rain-damp skirt and blouse, was zipping up an old, fuzzy green robe that felt warm and comforting on her chilled shoulders, when she heard a knock on her door. She grabbed a towel to dry her wet hair and went to answer it, sure it was her landlady bringing Puppy home—whenever it rained, Mrs. Langford always took Puppy into her kitchen. She flung the door wide, smiling, and took a step back.

"Oh," she said stupidly, "it's you."

Alec stared at her, taking in the robe and tangled hair, the look of shock.

"Who were you expecting?"

"P-Puppy."

"He knocks?"

Gail colored. "Mrs. Langford does. She keeps him in her place when it's raining." She tore her gaze away from his dark face and looked down at her old, faded robe. "I suppose I should put on a raincoat and go get him." Anything to cover up that horrible robe.

"I'll get him," Alec said. "I'm already wet."

"Oh, no..." Gail protested, but he was already gone, crashing through the shrubbery around the house. She gasped and flew to her bedroom to change.

Wearing jeans and a white pullover, Gail came back into the living room in time to see them come in. The Dobie bounced happily around Alec's tall, dripping figure.

"Your shirt is soaked," she said, sidestepping Puppy's headlong plunge at her legs. "Give it to me and I'll put it in the dryer. There are towels in the bathroom." She put out her hand, staring fixedly at his chin.

"Gail."

Unwillingly she raised her eyes to his. "Yes?"

"Are you telling me I can stay?"

She turned absolutely scarlet and let her hand drop. "I don't know what you mean, Alec."

He came close to her, grasping her shoulders, looking down at her without a trace of his usual amused smile. His strong hands felt solid and warm on her shoulders. His warm scent mingled with the cool scent of rain, and all she wanted was to move forward into his arms and breathe it in.

"Yes, you do," he said softly. "You know exactly what I mean, and you've had a week to make up your mind. Do you *want* me here?" He watched her gaze slide away from his face to the floor. He was pushing too hard. He knew it, but he had to know. Just seeing her laugh with that other man had shattered his confidence. Seeing her slim jaw tense before she answered didn't help, either.

"If you mean in my bed," Gail said resolutely, "no. Not yet. Otherwise, yes."

Alec's eyes widened, and then he laughed. *Not yet.* Her honesty was both funny and sweet. He pulled her into his arms and held her close, weak with relief. "That's plain enough, darling. I can wait—for a while." She felt so good, so soft and warm against his damp chest, her slim body relaxing against him, her arms sliding up around his neck. Kissing her, taking her mouth with a hunger he didn't try to hide, he felt the instant need that made them both strain closer, heard her little sigh, and knew he wouldn't have to wait long. He wans't sorry she had put him off. He wanted her to be sure from the first. He moved back, looking at her and frowning.

"I've gotten you wet," he said. Her white pullover was damp from his shirt. It clung to the high, rounded shapes of her breasts. Alec let out his breath and turned away.

"Better change, angel, if you want me to keep my hands to myself. I'll put my own shirt in the dryer."

She made coffee, adding the last of the brandy to the cups to ward off the chill of the rain. They drank it sitting in the small living room, talking of carefully impersonal things: of the weather—it looked like a chilly fall; of Alec's suddenly burgeoning practice—word had gotten around among the arthritic Florida retirees; and of Gail's new business enterprise. She had put up a sign at the Galleries offering her services as a certified interior decorator and already had several new clients.

"I should have done it before," Gail said. "It makes quite a difference to my income and works in well with the shop." She looked up and smiled at him. "The first time we met, you seemed to be saying I was hiding behind Lena and not trying hard enough. That was the push I needed. Thank you." She looked away again, rather quickly. Bare to the waist, Alec lounged in the chair across from her like a half-naked Greek god, his still-damp trousers clinging to his muscular thighs. The week apart hadn't helped those ridiculously wanton fantasies that kept invading her mind.

"The income isn't important," Alec said. He smiled at her quizzical look and added gently, "What's important is whether you like the work. Do you?"

"The extra money *is* important," Gail argued, "since I now need a car I can depend on." She curled back into her chair. "But of course I like doing it—it's fascinating to study the people who will be living in a place, then try to match colors and styles to them and the way they like to live."

"So you analyze your clients." Alec cocked a brow at her and grinned. "What are you going to do with my place?"

"Make it terrifically impressive and cool," Gail said, amused. "That will suit you very well."

"Ah. Should I feel complimented? What would you change if you were living there?"

Gail broke out in laughter. "I'd ruin it with a muddle of bookcases, potted plants, flowers and a large dog. I'm afraid I'm not very sophisticated."

"No," Alec said, "you're not, thank goodness." He got up and stretched, scanning her face as he did. "The bookcases can go along the east wall under the prints. The plants and flowers I'll leave to you. Puppy will be welcome anywhere upstairs. Downstairs, he might frighten the patients."

Gail stared at him, then laughed. "Now hold on," she said. "I live *here*. Even if I—we—well, whatever, I'm not going to move in with you."

He grinned and lifted her from her chair into his arms, holding her tightly against his bare chest, nuzzling her neck. "You think I'm suggesting this much too soon, don't you?"

"I certainly do. We don't—"

"Know each other well enough to live together," Alec finished for her, kissing his way from her neck to her mouth. "I have to agree. But I don't think we're going to need much time to get acquainted."

"This is ridiculous," Gail said faintly, "it really is...." Crushed against him, her hands on his bare back, she fought the spiraling warmth inside, the overwhelming wish to surrender to him. If he kept looking at her like that, she was going to agree to anything he said, so she turned and rested her cheek on his shoulder, closing her eyes. "Maybe you don't need time, but I do, Alec."

He was silent, rubbing his cheek on her hair. "I guess I can't fight that," he said finally. "If you're uncertain, I won't argue." He tipped her head back and kissed her again, gently, and let her down. "I'll get my shirt and say good-night. You've had a long day and it's late."

Gail stared after him as he went down the hall to the kitchen, thinking he must be crazy not to see how impossible it was. You just didn't move in with a stranger.

Not even if you felt you knew him better than you'd ever known anyone before.

Coming back up the hall, buttoning his shirt, Alec was shaky. He hadn't planned to say anything about living together; it had just come out, out of his desire and loneliness. He had an instinctive urge to hold on to her, to keep her for himself. Even marriage had flickered through his thoughts. All brought on, he decided, by the sight of that other man taking care of her, bringing her home in the rain.

Gail was still standing where he'd left her, looking confused and wary. He felt a guilty tenderness. "I'm sorry," he said, touching her cheek, "I guess I'm rushing you again."

Gail shook her head helplessly. "How could you take such a chance? You don't know me any better than I know you!"

"I know enough about you to know I need you in my life. All I'm asking is that you think about it. Will you?"

His gaze was so warm, searching her face, his voice so deep and sure. He *needed* her? Gail could feel her heart melting, running over. She glanced up again and nodded slowly. "Yes," she said, "of course I'll think about it. And you must, too. You'd be taking on more than just me, you know."

Alec grinned. "I do know. We'll spend Sunday morning with Dave and Ginny tomorrow, okay? I'll pick you up at nine." He swept her into his arms again and silenced the protest on her lips, kissing her with all his sensuous skill. She was breathless when he left, but so was he.

The rain had stopped, though tatters of dark clouds still drifted across the pale half-moon. Alec walked along the shining wet street and shivered, half from the cool air against his damp trousers and half from the sudden, fearful thought that Gail might turn him down, after all. For a woman like her, with conventional parents, a live-in arrangement was a big step. Maybe, in spite of what she had said and in spite of his own fears, he'd do better offering marriage. After all, as his friends had pointed out, a fair premarital agreement would prevent another disaster such as the one with Marian.

He pushed through the dripping bushes around the side of his house and went in the back door, running up the stairs. He switched on the lights and stood there, staring around the big room. Impressive and cool, she had said, and, dammit, she was right. It was almost sterile in effect, in spite of the colorful prints. It was cold. It badly needed the warmth Gail could give it, just as his life did.

5

"THERE'S JUST ONE THING," Gail said the next morning, settling herself and Puppy in the car, "I want you to promise me—"

"Not to let your parents guess I'm trying to lure you into my life," Alec supplied with a grin. Wearing jeans and a light chamois shirt, he appeared carefree and happy. "I promise. Anything else?"

Gail looked at him and laughed. "No, nothing more. You do know me, or maybe you just know my mother." She sat back and opened the window, threading her fingers through her freshly washed, still-damp hair and letting the breeze dry it. She felt wonderful, every inch of her gloriously alive. Laughter bubbled up in her throat. "Mom would lock me in the hall closet and lecture me through the door until I agreed to hold out for marriage. She's obsessed."

"She wants grandchildren."

Gail groaned. "You heard. She talks too much."

"I heard," Alec admitted serenely, "and I approve. As far as that goes, I think children are the only good reason to get married." He glanced over and caught Gail's startled look before she turned away to stare nonchalantly out the window. "You want children, don't you?"

"If and when I marry again," Gail said carefully, "I would like to have children." She looked back at him, suddenly curious. "Why? Would that be an issue with you?"

Alec smiled, his eyes on the road. "Not with you, since I know you want them, too."

"I'm not a candidate," Gail said dryly.

Alec grinned. "I can always hope, can't I? Anyway, children make a family."

Gail curled up in the seat and turned to face him, studying his strong, confident profile, the uptilted corner of his wide mouth. "So," she said lightly, "*you* have a list of requirements for marriage. What else is on it?"

Stopped at a red light, Alec looked over at her and recognized the challenge in her blue-eyed gaze. It was time to be diplomatic. He grinned. "I'm hard to please," he said. "If and when *I* marry, the woman has to have dark red hair, sky-blue eyes and a beautiful figure. She has to like children, dogs and me."

Gail laughed, relaxing. "In that order? Or would you rather be first?"

Alec laughed with her and shrugged. "Children and dogs are more endearing than most husbands," he said, driving on when the light changed. "However," he added, his tone altering slightly, "I would insist on being first, and *only*." He could feel Gail stiffen and go still. "I don't mean I think every woman plays around, but some couples now take that in stride, and it's not for me." He glanced at her again, taking in the outraged look on her face. "Naturally, I'd be the same. No other women."

She was silent as she stared out at the bright morning. Here was the bitterness in him, and now she thought she knew the reason. "Was your wife unfaithful, Alec?" she asked finally. "Is that why you think other women will be, too?"

Alec reddened. "A lot of women have their little affairs on the side. I suppose they get bored and look for something new." He hesitated, then reached for her hand, holding it in his as he drove. "We weren't talking about you, Gail. I didn't mean to imply that you were that kind."

He sounded, Gail thought, as if he meant to reassure her and himself. She felt a rush of sympathy. He was still raw inside, still hurting over his failed marriage. "Don't worry about it," she said, leaning back. "There are plenty of faithful women in the world. Most of them are if they know they're loved."

VIRGINIA WINSLOW greeted Alec like a long-lost son and turned a dancing, I-told-you-so eye on her daughter.

"Now I know it's serious," she said to Gail later, when they were alone. "You've brought him twice."

"I still don't have a car that runs," Gail said evasively. "And he does. But I'll have one next week. I've found a good buy at a secondhand lot. A wagon, so I can carry swatches and samples on my decorating jobs."

Virginia laughed. "A doctor's wife," she pointed out, "doesn't have to work. Stay home and have babies."

Gail sighed. "Did anyone ever tell you you're impossible?"

"Only your father."

"Add me to the list," Gail said absently, watching through the window as Alec and her father came back across the lawn, deep in conversation. There was no denying that both of her parents heartily approved of Alec. Her father's laughter boomed out at something

Alec said, and Virginia looked up, smiling when she saw them.

"David really enjoys having Alec here," she said. "He misses having a man to talk to since he retired. Most of our neighbors are old fogies who discuss nothing but their pains."

"Send them to me," Alec said, coming in in time to hear her last words. "Old fogy pains are my specialty." He was smiling and vibrant as he walked into the warm kitchen, bringing a drift of cool, fresh air in with him. His eyes lighted up when he saw Gail. Behind him, her father laughed again.

"He should have been a surgeon, Ginny. He cut a plank for me and he's mighty handy with a saw."

Gail shuddered. "Sawing off legs went out with Moby Dick, Dad. What's the plank for?"

"Bookcases," her father said proudly. "Alec's commissioned me to build a whole set of them. Which reminds me, your chest is finished. Want to take it home?"

"Certainly she does," Virginia broke in. "It's a hope chest, isn't it? She can start filling it."

"Alec," Gail said desperately, untying her apron, "let's go for a walk. You haven't seen much of the neighborhood yet."

Puppy went with them, his leash dangling from his long jaws. He stayed close to Gail when they passed one of the few houses, but ranged widely in the wooded sections. The air was still crisp in spite of the midmorning sun and they walked along the shell-surfaced road at a fast pace, talking and laughing until they were far past the last house.

"Beautiful land," Alec said, taking in the big trees and stretches of meadow. "Would you like to live out here?"

Gail smiled. "When I was a teenager that was my dream. A house in the country, kids, dogs and horses. I'm a lot more realistic now. Where I live is convenient to my work and very comfortable. And I can afford it."

Alec stopped. "Look at that over there," he said, facing her west. "The rolling land coming down from the woods to a little lake. There's a for sale sign on it."

Gail looked up at the sign, read the price and winced. Then she caught Alec's intent gaze and sighed. "You have a home," she reminded him gently. "A lovely home."

Alec laughed and they started walking again. "I know I do. But it's temporary. Eventually I plan to use the second floor as part of the office. And I've been wondering how to find the kind of land I want to build on. This seems ideal." He grinned down at her. "For one thing, you like it. You could have your horses."

"Good Lord," Gail said faintly. "Are you showing off or trying to bribe me?"

"Yes." He put his arm around her shoulders, pulling her close as they walked. "You bet I am. Both those things. Is it working?"

She looked up at his tanned, gleaming face, seeing the grin, the intent look in his hazel eyes. "Something is," she admitted, "but I'm not sure what."

Alec slowed, his grin fading. Then he bent suddenly and brushed a kiss on her ear. "I don't care what it is," he said huskily. "I'll take you any way I can get you. I need you, Gail, they way I need food and air. Don't leave me."

"Oh, Alec." She stopped, her eyes misting. "I won't. I really won't." She could feel his sincerity, and it seemed her heart had opened of its own accord and invited him in, whether she understood why or not. She drew a deep breath, pulled his head down and kissed him on the mouth. "Now," she said, trying for poise, "let's come down off this high and go back to the house."

Alec turned without a word and went with her toward her parents' house. He was amazed by what he had said, embarrassed by the way it had sounded. It had just come out, as if someone inside had said it, not him. He'd never needed anyone that much. What was the matter with him?

An hour later, Alec looked across the Winslows' dining table and caught Gail's attention. Clear, as blue as a summer sky, her eyes met his with tender warmth, without a trace of doubt or wariness. He sat still, absorbing the message and feeling his pulse accelerate, until Virginia forced him to notice the platter of chicken she was holding practically under his nose.

"Eat now," Virginia said, trying to keep her face straight, "look later."

Alec recovered with a laugh. "Good idea. But you'll have to admit your daughter has beautiful eyes."

"My daughter," Virginia said smugly, "is beautiful all over."

Mortified, Gail began toying with the food on her plate. Her mother was occasionally awful, but she loved her, anyway. Her father was sometimes stubborn and cranky, and she loved him. Alec was an idealistic but bitter and puzzling man, and she loved *him*. It was hard to believe she had fallen in love so fast, but she had. After a while she glanced up and caught his gaze on her again, intimate and supremely confident. *He knows*, she thought. *He knows he's won.* She smiled, not minding a bit, and watched his sensual mouth soften into a slow grin as he pushed his chair back and stood.

"Wonderful dinner, Ginny. I hope you won't mind if I become a regular Sunday visitor."

"I'll be hurt if you don't," Virginia said, rising to clear the table. "More pie?"

"Keep it for Dave's midnight foray," Alec answered. "May I use your telephone?"

"Of course." Virginia waved a slender hand toward David's study and looked questioningly at Gail when he left. "Checking on a patient, do you suppose?"

"Hmm? Oh. I don't know, Mom." Gail rose hurriedly, clattering the dishes as she picked them up. "Let's get this done. He may want to leave early." She caught a cup as it started to slip and balanced it on top of a stack of plates, then headed for the kitchen.

Virginia followed, staring. "Are you all right?"

"Hmm? Oh. I . . ."

"'Hmm, oh' yourself," Virginia said, and laughed. "Be careful with my china. What have you two been up to?"

"What makes you think we've been up to something?" Gail asked weakly.

"Forget I said that." Still grinning, Virginia began loading the dishwasher. "I'll try again. What happened?"

The dishwasher was humming when Alec came into the kitchen to collect Gail. "Sorry to drag your daughter away," he told Virginia, "but there's someone I have to see."

"Good," Virginia said cheerfully. "Maybe you can make her talk. I certainly can't."

"I swear that next week she'll buy a rack and some thumbscrews," Gail said outside. "What a nosy woman!" She let Puppy into the car, then got in, too, and busied herself with his leash as Alec started the car

and they drove off. Relieved to have escaped her
mother's unremitting prying, she sank into the seat,
pushing back flyaway hair from her flushed face. Then
a road sign caught her eye and she shot bolt upright.
"Wait. This is the wrong way, Alec."

Alec laughed. "No, it's the right way. We're meeting
a real estate agent at the acreage by the lake. If it's what
we want I'll nail it down."

"You're putting me on. This is Sunday."

"Real estate agents in Florida don't take time off.
They sleep fully clothed, clutching their briefcases,
ready day or night to leap up and grab the unwary
buyer. When I called, this one was both willing and eager to tramp through the woods with us."

"Good grief," she said faintly. "You've lost your
mind."

"Oh, no." At ease in the big bucket seat, the breeze
ruffling his bronze hair, Alec chuckled. "I know what
I want." His gaze slid over her, warmly approving.
"Besides, think what I'll save with an in-house decorator."

As much as she disapproved of his brashness, his
carefree assumption that she would fall in with his plans
and accept his proposal, Gail couldn't help but laugh.
In spite of the few silver hairs at Alec's temples, he
looked like a small boy on Christmas Eve. Excited and
happy, bubbling with enthusiasm. How could she argue with that?

They tramped the perimeter of the five acres, following the pudgy agent, who pointed out the sur-
veyor's marks, led them cannily through the big,
handsome trees and brought them down across the
gently rolling meadow to the serene little lake. A pair
of brightly colored wood ducks flew up as if on cue,

circled the lake, then came down again to paddle around and watch the humans with beady, inquisitive eyes.

Standing on the small sandy beach, the agent took out a handkerchief and wiped his sweating forehead. "Pretty," he said with admirable restraint. "Prime land, good view. Utilities underground along the road—wouldn't cost much to bring them in. What do you think?"

"Who's handling the land on the other side of the lake?" Alec asked, squinting at it. "It looks low."

"We are. And you're right, it is low. Has to be filled to build on it. It's a two acre tract." The agent gazed at Alec thoughtfully. "If you took both pieces of land, we'd let you have the second for another eight thousand. Cheap enough, right?"

"Six," Alex said, "and I'll sign now."

"Done. I've got some blank contracts in the car."

Speechless, Gail followed them back to the road and sat with Puppy in the BMW while the business was transacted on the hood of the realtor's wagon. Watching Alec as he bent to scrawl his name on a fluttering paper, she wondered if he always made up his mind so fast, and if he ever regretted it. Then she saw him shake hands with the agent and head back to the car, his wind-whipped hair glinting in the sun, his superbly proportioned body accented by the clinging chamois shirt and tight jeans. He flashed a grin as he opened the door and slid in beside her.

"One teenage dream coming up," he said, and pulled her into his arms. He tasted of fresh air and excitement, of desire and triumph. When he let her go she was limp and breathless, her ravished mouth a deep pink. She laughed a little, catching her breath.

"Don't you dare blame my dreams for that extravagant gesture," she said. "It would have taken me months to make up my mind to buy that land, even if I'd had the money. You decided in a second."

Alec laughed. "But look at it, darling. It's beautiful and it's ours. Why wait? Someone else might get it."

"It's yours," Gail corrected. "Not ours."

"Same thing," Alec said carelessly, and started the car. "Let's go home and celebrate."

They took the Dobie to Gail's place and the walled yard, and provided him with fresh water. Then at Alec's house they went up the stairs with their arms around each other. "The rug I ordered is in," Alec said. "And you're the first guest. See how you like it." He threw open the door with a flourish and ushered her in.

"You found the perfect color." Gail moved from the small entrance onto the lush blue rug and sank down in the middle of it. Looking up at him, she laughed. "Soft as lamb's wool and the same shade of blue as a peacock's feathers. What luxury, Alec."

Alec dropped down beside her. "I'm glad you approve. I had to pick it out alone, since you were so busy thinking last week." He leaned back on his elbows and stared at her with a faint smile. "You look wonderful surrounded by Persian blue, angel. It makes your hair glow like fire."

Gail shook back her hair and stretched out beside him, propping her head on her hand and eyeing him teasingly. "Now that's what I call flattering. You planned your color scheme around me."

His gaze played warmly over her animated face, the graceful curves of her reclining figure. He reached for her and pulled her to him with a smile. "Of course I did.

I even told the painters my woman had dark red hair and blue, blue eyes, and they took it from there."

Gail's laughter died away. His woman. Her man. Could it be as simple as that? She reached up and stroked his dark, firm cheek, her eyes jewellike and gleaming in the soft light. "What makes you think I'm your woman?"

"This," Alec said huskily, and he bent to take her lips with an exquisite gentleness, nudging them apart with the tip of his tongue. His hands cupped the sides of her head; his warm, hard chest pressed lightly against her breasts. His lips clung for a moment, then began moving with sensual slowness over the soft fullness of her mouth. Gail let out her breath softly and yielded to the delicious feeling, her tongue curling to touch his, coaxing it into her mouth with little licks. Sudden heat flashed between them like a bolt of lightning, jolting them both. Alec groaned and tightened his hold on her. "See?" he asked hoarsely. "This doesn't lie."

Gail wasn't sure of that. Passion could lie. But she was sure she loved him, sure she wanted him. She was burning with desire, her loins pooling with liquid heat, her breasts pressing against his chest with taut, aching nipples. Her wide eyes searched his face, tight with passion, then drifted away, her thick lashes fluttering down to lie like fans against the flushed ivory of her cheeks.

"Your woman," she whispered huskily. "That's what I want to be."

Alec caught his breath. Was it happening now? Another woman might say that to lead him on, but Gail said what she meant. "Look at me," he said, "and say that again."

She could feel the strong beat of his heart against her breasts, feel the heat and hardness of his body against her side. She opened her eyes and looked at him, and the air around them seemed to pulsate. "I want," she said, sliding her arms around his neck, "I truly want to be your woman."

For an instant his expression was triumphant, and then his eyes became misty with tenderness. He touched her face gently, sweeping a lock of hair back from her smooth forehead. "Now, darling?"

"Yes, now," she said softly.

He stood swiftly with that animal grace she so loved and pulled her to her feet. "Then you shall be," he whispered. "My woman, now and forever."

Alec carried her into his bedroom, where only the small lamp over a framed print provided light. The room was done in shades of gray, from the charcoal rug to the smoky silk draperies. To Gail, the air seemed to swirl with soft gray fog as he began to undress her. When she tried to help, he took her hands in his and kissed them, his tongue hot on her slender palms, his teeth nipping her fingertips.

"Let me," he said softly. "This first time. I want to do it all. I've dreamed of it, angel."

She loved him, so what he wanted she wanted. She stood still while his agile fingers unbuttoned, unzipped, unsnapped and drew off her shirt and her bra, her shoes and the soft, worn jeans. He told her how lovely she was, his voice a husky murmur, his hands adoring her body, cupping her small, round breasts, sliding slowly down the curves that led to her narrow waist and the smooth flare of her hips. His mouth followed his hands, leaving a warm, moist trail that made her shudder with desire. Then, when he sat on his heels to draw down her thin silk panties, he leaned forward and kissed the satin skin below her navel, grasping her buttocks in his palms and holding her close as he moved down to tongue the center of her triangle of chestnut curls. Gail gasped and balanced herself with her hands on his shoulders, her slender thighs trembling.

"Please, no."

"For my woman, yes," Alec said hoarsely. "For my woman, everything." Then he flung back the brilliant blue throw on the bed and lifted her onto the cool white sheets.

Gail's eyes were full of passion as she watched him take off his clothes. She had admired his body from a distance and in her dreams, but now her fantasies were real. When she saw his golden-tan torso emerge from his white shirt, the shadowy light accenting the ripple of strong muscles across his shoulders and back, her mouth went dry and her already racing pulse quickened. Then, as he unbuckled his belt and slid out of his slacks, the sight of his powerful loins and full arousal flooded her with an almost painful rush of desire. She held out her arms to him, drawing him close as he slipped onto the bed beside her.

"Let me?" she whispered, touching him lightly, looking into his eyes.

Alec looked back, staring into deep, glowing, indigo blue. Then, in answer, he stretched his big body full length and lay still. "Yes, make love to me, angel. Show me you want me. I need to know that."

Was there a trace of bitterness in the last words, the trace of an old hurt? Whatever it might be, Gail wanted passionately to drive it away, to fill him with her love. She leaned over him, her breasts resting softly against his chest, and began with parted lips and a flicking

tongue to tease his mouth, his ears, his strong, mus-
cled neck.

"I don't know what this is doing to you," she whispered, "but I know what it's doing to me. Don't ask me
to stop." She was acutely aware of his dark male scent,
the faintly salty, musky taste of his skin, and the tex-
ture, first bristly against her tongue, then as she moved
downward smooth and hard. She nuzzled the haze of
golden hair on his chest, found a flat nipple and kissed
it until it hardened, then followed the narrowing line
of crisp curls to his flat belly and tongued his navel. She
was immersed in him, swimming in sensation, feeling
his hands on her back press her closer as she moved on.

"Angel," Alec murmured, "I warn you . . . you're
driving me crazy. That's enough." He grasped her waist
and lifted her, looking at her flushed and sensuous face,
the dreaming, dark blue eyes and moist, parted lips.
And he realized that behind her seeming naïveté, hidden inside that neat, slender body, was far more passion than he had ever thought. He eased her down
beside him and turned to pull her tight against the wall
of his big body.

"Let *me*," he whispered, and bent to the straining tips
of her breasts, smoothing his hand down to the apex of
her thighs, searching out the heated, moist flesh he
knew he would find.

Gail buried her fingers in his hair, holding him as she
pressed her breasts into the hot cavern of his mouth and
arched shamelessly against his probing hand. When she
saw him swing himself up and hover over her, she made
small, urgent sounds and lifted her slender hips to take
him in.

Alec entered her carefully, slowly, but when the hot,
wet velvet of her flesh enclosed him and tightened with

need, his control broke in a storm of passion. The thick muscles of his powerful back sprang to life beneath her hands. He took her supple, rippling body with long, hard thrusts, and she clung to him in rapturous, rolling embraces that left them breathless and gasping, helplessly laughing as they came perilously close to the edge of the bed.

"You'll have me on the floor," Gail warned, choking on laughter as she wriggled away to safety.

"Just so I have you," Alec growled. "I don't care where."

Then, as if some subtle signal passed between them, they gentled together into a swinging, soaring rhythm that built a wave of exquisite tension that crested, then broke in a tumult of ecstasy.

Drifting down slowly from the peak of pleasure, they ended in an exhausted tangle of glowing bodies, legs and arms seeming inextricably mixed. Eyes closed, Gail returned to the world at the sound of Alec's voice.

"It's true," he said unevenly. "The poets are right, after all. Some people are made for each other."

Gail was silent. She lay looking at him with her eyes filled with wonder. She had loved Bob, and she had enjoyed the pleasant lovemaking that had made her feel close and secure with him. But this . . . Her eyes went past Alec's broad, gleaming shoulder and fastened on the lighted print she had never seen before. It was done in shades of gray, like the room, and depicted a great storm at sea, a battle of wind and waves. Alec was like the racing dark clouds, the whirl of shattering wind, and she had been like the usually calm sea, wakened and brought to life by his force, rising with a surging, exulting need to meet him. She closed her eyes again, half-frightened by her thoughts, wondering if she would be strong enough for the turbulence of loving him.

"Married as soon as we can arrange it," Alec was saying, and Gail's eyes flew open.

"What did you say?"

He chuckled, stretching out luxuriously and pulling her close to lie with her head on his shoulder. "A fine thing. I propose to you and you aren't even listening. I said we'd be married as soon as we could. There's no reason now to wait."

For a moment Gail was silent. It seemed to her that her love for Alec was a thing apart, a new and powerful emotion that had nothing to do with the thoughtful planning of a marriage, a home together, duties and children. At least not yet. Maybe soon, when they thoroughly understood each other, they could think about it. Certainly not this minute. She twisted to look up at him.

"There's no reason *not* to wait," she said softly. "We have each other now. We can see how we get along together before we get married."

Alec stared, incredulous, then laughed and hugged her. "We'll get along, angel. How can we miss? We need each other. I'll take the chance if you will." His gaze, roaming her irresolute face, was very confident.

Gail stared back at him, the wonderful feeling of sensual bliss gradually fading, leaving her mind clear. Maybe too clear. Alec was too offhand. There was something missing, some part of him still closed off and hidden from her, even now, when they'd been as close as two people could be. She looked away and sat up, slid from the bed and began picking up her clothes.

"But I won't," she said firmly. "Marriage is too important to take chances. Later, we'll know."

"Gail!" He was out of bed and wrapping her in his arms, his face stricken. "Darling, we're perfect together. What's wrong?"

She shook her head, confused again as she felt herself melting against him, felt their heartbeats quicken and drum together, and then, incredulously, felt the strong new stirring of his loins and the answering heat in her own. "I don't know," she whispered. "But I guess it isn't this...."

6

STARING ACROSS Alec's wide chest at the bedside clock, Gail groaned. "It's after midnight—no, it's after one! I have to go home."

"Why?"

She laughed and slid away from him, landing on her feet in the thick charcoal rug. "Because I live there and I don't want to shock Mrs. Langford at dawn."

Alec stood and reached for his clothes. "See how much better it would be if we were married?"

As she buttoned her shirt, Gail smiled. "You don't have to get up, Alec. It's only a block."

"Which I will walk with you. In the absence of Puppy, I am your guard." He grinned at her and rumpled her already tangled hair. "No argument allowed. Besides, I'm hungry. Do you have any eggs? I know how to cook eggs."

Gail chuckled. "Now there's an example—how can you want to marry me without knowing if *I* can cook, too?"

"After tonight how can you ask?"

Sitting in her warm kitchen later, watching Alec devour a huge mound of scrambled eggs, bacon and toast and feeding Puppy portions from her own plate, Gail felt cozily domestic. Relaxed and pleasantly tired in the afterglow of lovemaking, she thought how wonderfully satisfying it would be to be married to this man she loved, even if she never really understood him. Maybe she was being too cautious. But still . . .

"Alec," she said curiously, "we've known each other only a little over two weeks. How can you be so sure our marriage would be a success?"

"Because you make marvelous scrambled eggs?"

"I'm serious."

"All right." He pushed back his chair and gave Puppy the last bit of bacon from his plate. "Then I'll be serious. I'm *not* sure. Marriage is always a gamble, darling, after two weeks or two years." He looked away, his heavy gold brows knit, and absently stroked the Dobie's sleek head. "Or ten years," he added flatly. "I found that out the hard way. Maybe people change—or maybe they marry for the wrong reasons. I don't know. Hell, I don't even know if you'd be happy with me." He looked up with a faint smile. "But I do know one thing—I want you in my life. You're the one who has to decide if you want me in yours."

For once Gail knew that he spoke from deep conviction, that he meant exactly what he said. She felt she'd been given a glimpse into his hidden nature—certainly not all the way, but enough to begin to understand him. He was a very complex, very hurt man beneath his charming surface.

"That's clear," she said slowly. "Thanks for telling me how you feel." She slid out of her chair and began clearing the table, running hot water in the sink to wash the few dishes.

"I'll help," Alec said gruffly, and came to her, grabbing a dish towel. "I've kept you up too late."

They finished in silence, but at the door Alec tipped her face up to his and kissed her lightly, his usual ironic smile in place.

"Did I ruin my chances with you, darling?"

"No." She was surprised to feel the heat of tears in her eyes. "I can't make decisions as quickly as you do, Alec, and it will take time for me to really consider that much of a change. But I think when I do answer you, it'll be yes. You're already in my life, and there'd be a big empty space if you left."

"Thank God," Alec said softly, and kissed her again. "Now go to bed and get some rest. I'll see you tomorrow."

Alec walked home on air. She was all he had hoped for and so much more. A lovely, passionate woman. But amazingly stubborn. Still, he was sure she would give in once they knew each other better. Which reminded him that he'd better see a lawyer.

THE NEXT SIX WEEKS were the happiest, most fulfilling weeks of Gail's life. She stopped trying to hide her love for Alec from her parents and Lena. It would have been impossible, anyway; when she and Alec weren't working, they were together.

"Get married," Virginia commanded in private. "He'll make a lovely father."

Gail laughed. "Can't you think of anything else but grandchildren and weddings?"

Virginia laughed. "Get the priorities straight. Wedding first."

Gail smiled and let the remarks pass. Virginia's nagging had never really bothered her, and now in her new, strong confidence she saw only the love behind it. Truthfully, she was too happy to care, for many reasons. Alec was the main reason, of course, but she was growing in another way. She had bought the car she wanted and her popularity as an interior decorator was rising quickly. She had more jobs than she could handle, and her feelings of self-worth had doubled along with her skills. She bought new and becoming clothes, trained another assistant for Lena and took off on her own. Alec was intensely proud of her, and one evening as they relaxed in his big living room he told her so.

"You have a wonderful feeling for places and people, darling. I'm impressed with what you're doing with Van Loessen's house. You don't like formality yourself, but you knew they'd love it—and they do. And look at this place since we put in the bookcases and your 'muddle' of plants and new lamps. It's a home—or it would be, if you'd just move in."

Gail smiled, warmed by his praise. They were sitting together on his long, low sofa, their feet propped carelessly on a coffee table while they sipped hot-buttered rum at the end of a cold, rainy evening. The draperies were drawn and the room glowed with soft lights and muted color. She looked at the two Bleeker prints of hot summer days on the beach and remembered the afternoon she had brought them here. It seemed long ago in another life.

"Lately I'm here more often than at my place," she pointed out. "Doesn't that count?"

Alec slanted a look at her. She seemed perfectly contented, her eyes warmly adoring as she gazed at him. "You know what I want from you," he said. "Just slow down from all your dashing around and say the right word. Or are you still uncertain?"

Gail looked away, peering into the mug she held and thinking hard. She knew now why she kept putting him off, but she hadn't had the courage to bring it up. It would sound so juvenile. But still, she had to tell him at some point.

"Do you realize," she said softly, "that in all this time you've never said you loved me?" She looked up at him and caught the tremor of tension that rippled along his jaw. "I know that sounds childish, as if it took words to make it real. But . . . maybe it does. I love you, Alec. Do you love me?"

The illusion called love. He wasn't ready for this moment of truth. But he didn't want to lie to her, either. He forced a smile and put down his mug.

"You're right," he said, "it does sound childish. Words are nothing. It's action that counts." He took her mug from her and put it beside his. "Let me show you how I feel, darling."

She protested, but her words were muffled by his seeking mouth. She struggled a bit, but the fire between them never went out; it was only banked into glowing coals. Their passion for each other had grown steadily since that first night, and by now it took only a touch or a certain look to bring them together. In moments they were struggling with their clothes instead of each other, a murmurous, gasping, half-laughing tangle of two heated bodies on the long sofa. Clothes flew through the air, were pushed up and pulled down, were dropped to the floor.

"Crazy man," Gail whispered breathlessly. "There's a bed in the other room."

Alec's answer was a growl and an accurate thrust of his loins that took the rest of her breath away. "Oh, Alec," she gasped, "oh, darling . . ." Surrender was sweet.

THE RAIN HAD STOPPED when it was time for Gail to go home, but the air was damp and cold. Alec gave her one of his sweaters, which hung to her hips, and walked with her to her house, coming in to make sure the heat was on. Gail pulled off the sweater and gave it to him.

"I appreciate all this TLC," she said, kissing him lightly. "But I can take care of myself. I've been doing it for years."

"I'm taking over," he said, then reached into the inner pocket of his jacket and brought out a long, over-size envelope. "I want you to read this when you're alone. And, please, think about it seriously. Promise?"

"Of course," Gail said, looking curiously at the envelope. "If that's what you want." She noticed he looked tense. "What is it?"

"You'll see, darling. I think you'll approve, but you'll need to let your attorney read it before you sign it. You'll note that I already have."

"Sign it?" She laughed uncertainly. "An attorney? Now wait . . . What is this, really? Stay and explain."

"No. It's something your attorney can explain better than I can. Good night, darling. See you tomorrow."

Puzzled, she watched him leave, shutting the door firmly behind him. By habit, she walked to the door and locked it, then, looking at the envelope again, she went to her favorite chair and sat down to find out what was in it.

The envelope contained two copies of what seemed to be some kind of contract, judging from the "whereas" and "therefore" legal language she always had trouble following. There was also a handwritten note, which she read first. *Darling, this may make our marriage less of a gamble for us both. If there is anything in it that troubles you, I'm open to suggestions. Alec.*

What in the world? She laid aside the note, took one of the copies and began reading. She had heard of premarital agreements, but this was the first she had ever seen. After the first explanatory paragraph, which was plain enough, the document began a listing of what Alec Morgan—the party of the first part, for heaven's sake!—contracted to provide for Gail Winslow Sheridan—party of the second part—when in due course they were married.

Gail read on, increasingly confused. A home. A car. She *had* a car! A household allowance and a personal allowance, both ridiculously large, far more than anyone needed. She skipped through the ponderous language, picking out parts. All medical expenses. An equal voice in decisions concerning the family. Yearly vacations. Emotional support. *Emotional support?*

She turned to the second page, biting her lip. Gail Winslow Sheridan, party of the second part, evidently was to oversee the maintenance of the home, share responsibility for the care of Bruce Morgan, son of Alec Morgan by a former marriage, and the care of any children born of this union. She would also oversee meals, with the assistance of a cook and other household employees she would choose. Gail Winslow Sheridan, Gail thought wryly, was going to have it easy.

Moving from shock to a clear feeling of unreality, Gail went on to read the last paragraph, a bewildering maze of legal terms, from which she gathered that both parties agreed that whatever monies and properties they individually possessed at the time of their marriage would not thereafter be considered joint or communal properties as in the usual marriage, but would remain in their original ownership. Therefore, the document continued delicately, each party renounced any claim on the monies and properties of the other in the event that the marriage ended in divorce. Furthermore, in that case, custody of any and all children of the union would be held by the parent deemed best able to provide for them financially. Visitation rights would be arranged for the other parent.

That was it. Gail sat there, staring at the paper, listening to the heavy thump of her heart in silence. She felt shamed, accused of some crime she didn't understand. Yet there was Alec's firm signature, witnessed and notarized, and a place for her signature and another notary seal. Tears blurred her eyes as she folded the sheets and put them back in the envelope.

It wasn't that she didn't understand why Alec had done it; she understood too well. He wanted her enough to offer her the moon, but he had no faith in the marriage lasting. He was armoring himself against an expected disaster. Deep inside, he must believe he had to protect his fortune and his future children from her.

Staring at his signature, Gail was sure she knew why. It was because once another woman had deceived him. In a way, she thought, he was still firmly tied to his ex-wife by... what? Love or hate? Actually, it made no difference to Gail which it was. Because on those pages it was clearly shown that Alec didn't trust *her*. And where there was no trust, there could be no real love.

IN THE MORNING Gail sealed the envelope, wrote Alec's name on it and labeled it "Personal." Then she took it to his house and left it with old Miss Pennington to give to him.

"Any message?" Penny asked curiously.

Gale hesitated. "No," she said finally. "He won't need a message. He'll understand without one."

Back at her place, Gail got into her station wagon, loaded in Puppy and took off for her parents' house.

She knew what she wanted to do now. When Bob had drowned she'd learned to dull pain with hard, constant work. And in spite of the fact that she understood Alec's problem, this was pain, too.

She was thankful for the backlog of clients and the long hours that would help keep her mind occupied. Good for her, but not for the Dobie, lonesome at home. He, she had decided, would visit for a while with her parents. He'd be happier with them than alone in the evenings.

"Of course we'll keep him," Virginia said a half hour later, stroking the Dobie's sleek coat. "We both love Puppy. But why this sudden decision to work twelve hours a day? If you need money—"

"It isn't that," Gail interrupted hastily. "I don't need anything. I'm just . . . behind schedule." Standing beside her car, she looked pale and tired in the bright morning sun. "If you're sure you don't mind keeping my dog . . ."

"I mind the way you look," her mother said sharply. "What's wrong? You look like you've lost your last friend."

Irritation leapt up in Gail, then disappeared as she saw the concern in Virginia's green eyes. "Never will I lose my last friend," she said, and gave her mother a quick hug. "Not while I still have you." She patted Puppy and got back into the car. "You stay," she told the dog firmly. "I'll be out Sunday."

One of Gail's waiting clients was a builder, Sam Ormond, who was remodeling an immense old house into a series of apartments. Nothing was standardized. Windows were assorted shapes and sizes; floor spaces varied wildly. Gail went there next. Amid the banging of hammers and buzzing of saws, she asked for a key to the place.

"I can work here evenings when the carpenters are gone, measuring and planning for the draperies and rugs," she told the builder. "I'll be able to give you a price sooner, and it'll shorten the decorating time after the remodeling is done."

Surprised but pleased, Ormond gave her a key. "Sure you want to be here alone at night?" he asked. "There's no one living in any of these old houses around here."

"That won't bother me," Gail assured him. "I'll be too busy to think about it." Too busy, she hoped, to think about anything but the job at hand. Tucking the key in her purse, she glanced at her watch. She was due at a private home at ten, and it was already after nine. Just time enough, if she hurried, to pick up the sketches and samples she'd left on her kitchen table. She drove rapidly toward Charlotte Street, her pale face tense but determined.

Skidding to a stop in front of her place, she swung the car door wide, leaving it open, and half ran up the walk. Alec was standing at her door, the oversize envelope in one hand. He turned at the sound of her quick tapping heels.

"There you are," he said, frowning but relieved, "I thought I'd missed you."

Gail came to a dead stop, feeling as if she'd run into a wall. She'd hoped to put off seeing him at least for a day, longer if she could, long enough to harden her resolve. She stared at him, jolted by pain and a rising anger. How *dare* he act as if nothing had changed?

"I haven't time to talk," she said stiffly. "Please go away."

Alec's frown deepened. "No. Your clients can wait until we straighten this out." He came down the steps and took her arm. "Come on. We'll talk inside."

The warmth of his hand, his scent, his nearness and her love for him brought a new and agonizing rush of pain. Her eyes filled with tears. "Don't do this to me," she said unevenly. "I've nothing to say to you."

"Gail!" His arms went around her, crushing her close. "Don't do this to *us*. Just tell me what bothered you so much." He leaned back and looked at her, his anxious eyes searching her face. "You owe me that, don't you?"

"I don't owe you anything," Gail said, but she went with him, allowing him to lead her up the steps. She unlocked the door and went in, setting her jaw and evading him as he followed and reached for her again.

"All right," she said, "I suppose we have to talk. Let's get it over with." She took one of the chairs, glad to get off her shaking legs. After a moment of hesitation, Alec sat down opposite her.

"I guess I was wrong," he began, trying to be calm. "I thought you'd be pleased with this agreement. I felt you needed to feel secure about our marriage, and I tried to be generous. But from the way you're taking this, evidently you think I was trying to—to put something over on you."

"Weren't you?" Her blue eyes, startling in her white face, came up and met his. "Didn't you think if you offered me all that money and easy living I'd stop asking for love and trust and fall into your arms?" She watched the guilty flush suffuse his tanned face, watched him struggle to keep his eyes on hers, and the last, faint hope in her heart withered and died. That had been exactly what he'd thought.

"I love you," she added quietly, "but I'm not going to marry you. You're still married to another woman."

Alec stiffened. "You're crazy," he said harshly, "I *hate* Marian. Not because she left me, but because of her complete disloyalty and the way she robbed me of my son! She has nothing to do with this."

"She has everything to do with it," Gail said. "You wrote that agreement for her, not me." From somewhere she found the strength to stand up and leave him. She made her way down the hall to the kitchen, coming back with her arms full of the materials she'd need for the morning's job.

Alec was up, pacing the floor. He swung around and faced her. "In a way," he said painfully, "I suppose you're right. I'm trying to protect myself from losing again. It's damn near killed me not having Bru, and I couldn't stand having it happen twice. I've offered you everything I have. I'm sure your attorney will tell you it's more than fair."

Gail's heart hurt for him as much as for herself. She wished she could put her arms around him and tell him she loved him enough for both of them. But that wouldn't be true. She needed his love, too, and his trust. She couldn't settle for less.

"I'm sorry, Alec. I think I understand, but it doesn't help." She tried to smile, and made a miserable job of it. "I'm even greedier than you thought—I wanted *you*. All of you, not just the outside. Anyway, I'm leaving— I'm late for my appointment. And you must have patients waiting."

He glanced at his watch and nodded. Helping her into her car outside, he looked a little more confident.

"We'll work it out, darling. I'll see you this evening."

Gail drove away without answering. She intended to work late enough that he'd give up waiting. Why talk again? There weren't any words either one of them could honestly say that would change anything.

7

LEAVING HER DAY'S WORK at five o'clock, Gail found a small, out-of-the-way restaurant and had dinner then drove through the early fall twilight to Ormond's apartment project and let herself in. Even with the place brightly lighted, the absence of other people was disconcerting as night fell. The old floors creaked and her footsteps echoed in the empty rooms; the windows were black holes in the night. Her skin crawled as she remembered the flimsy lock on the front door.

Shaking off her apprehension, Gail reminded herself that there was nothing, really, to attract criminals to this deserted neighborhood. She forced herself to ignore the eerie sounds and loneliness and concentrated on measuring the windows and drawing her diagrams of window treatments.

At midnight she had finished her plans for two of the large apartments on the first floor. Her eyes drooping with weariness, she packed up her drawing pads and notes and left, turning off all the lights and making her way along the long, uneven path from the house to the dimly lighted street. She stumbled in the darkness and blamed herself—why in the world hadn't she thought to bring a flashlight?

As she drove home, she promised herself she'd be more efficient the following night. A flashlight, a thermos of coffee, a cup—things night owls needed. Turning onto Charlotte Street, she saw a muted glow from the long windows on the top of Alec's house and her throat tightened. Still up, at almost one a.m.—late, for a man who rose before dawn. She drove into the alley on the south side of the house where she lived, parked and got out, letting herself into the walled yard and through the back door. If Alec looked from his windows he could see the lights come on in her living room, so she left them off, creeping through the black hall to her bedroom.

As she lay in bed after her shower, Gail knew she had been a coward to sneak in. But she wasn't at all sure she could hold out in another confrontation with Alec. If he touched her . . . if he kissed her . . . She groaned and sat up, punched her pillow into shape and flung herself down again. *Go to sleep. Tomorrow there will be another job. Tomorrow and tomorrow . . . oh, Lord, all the tomorrows without him.*

DRIVING AWAY the next morning, Gail looked in her rearview mirror and saw Alec, his bronze hair and tanned skin washed with gold from the slanting rays of the sun. He was striding purposefully from his house toward her front door. She drove on, glancing back once as she turned the corner and seeing that he had stopped short and was staring after her. She forced herself to go on, swallowing the pain in her throat. He'd give it up after a while. His pride wouldn't let him go on trying. Somehow the thought wasn't much of a comfort.

Today she was finishing the last touches in the Van Loessen mansion. There had been a wait for one set of draperies and an old oil painting she was having cleaned and reframed at Coleman's. She went to the drapery shop first, then to Coleman's, stopping on the way to pick up Lena's favorite Danish pastries.

Ruth, the new assistant, met her at the door, smiled at the sight of the pastry box and hurried to the back room to make extra coffee. Lena looked up from polishing the ornate gilt frame for the Van Loessen painting and beamed.

"Wait until your classy client sees this," she bragged. "They'll never recognize the murky old landscape they had.... What's the matter with *you*, Gail? You look worn out."

"Lack of sleep," Gail said shortly, studying the painting. "I'm working overtime, playing catch-up. The painting looks wonderful, Lena. Bright and new. The Van Loessens will be pleased."

"Then you *are* working nights." Lena put the painting down and reached for the box of Danish. "Come on back and have a cup of coffee with us. Maybe it'll perk you up." Leading the way, she went on chatting. "Sam Ormond told me you were spending the evenings at his new project, but I hardly believed it. You shouldn't push yourself that hard."

"I know," Gail said, thinking how much Lena sounded like her mother. "But I was falling behind." She sat down, grateful for the coffee and the friendship. "It won't kill me, you know. And I like getting those dangling jobs done."

Lena shrugged. "It won't help. There'll just be more. I have four new clients for you to call when you have time."

"Sounds wonderful." It did. Relaxing in the company of the two women, Gail felt less alone. All three of them were working for a living; all three of them were widows and had much the same problems. Lena was glad to take calls for Gail and set up appointments. It benefited her business of selling decorative art. And Ruth, in her first job since her husband had died, was immensely thankful to them both. It was good, Gail reflected, to be with friends. And the new jobs would help her to keep busy.

Lena finished one pastry and reached for another. "You may think it's wonderful to work day and night, but I'll bet Alec Morgan will object, if he hasn't already."

Gail put down her half-eaten Danish, drained her cup and rose, forcing a smile. "The Van Loessens will be the ones objecting if I don't show up on time," she said lightly. "See you later."

In the outer room she slipped the renewed painting into a large paper bag and took it out to her car, her hands shaking as she put it carefully in the back seat. Even the mention of Alec had hurt, twisting her insides and ruining the few moments of companionship she had felt. She should have eaten the rest of that pastry, at least. She wasn't eating enough, and what sleep she had managed had been fitful. A very old, very tired cliché came to her mind: When the going gets tough, the tough get going.

"So, get going," she said half-aloud.

THAT EVENING, she lingered over her dinner at an obscure restaurant, making herself finish the steak she had ordered and the last bit of salad. She'd spent part of her lunch hour shopping for a big flashlight and a thermos, and before she left the restaurant she had the thermos filled with coffee. Armed with these, her notebooks and drawing pad, she drove to Ormond's apartments again.

She left the downstairs dark when she arrived and used her flashlight to climb the long flight of stairs to the second floor. Again she was conscious of the loneliness, the eerie sounds, compounded tonight by a gusting wind that rattled the shutters and set tree branches scraping against the sides of the house. Reminding herself that neither wind nor noises would hurt her, she turned on all the upstairs lights and looked around. Three smaller apartments, and the windows even more oddly shaped and mismatched than the others. All right, a challenge, then. She turned off the lights in two of the apartments to spare expense for Sam, set up her pad and notebook on a carpenter's table in the third and began the tedious job of measuring.

An hour or so later she poured a cup of coffee and sat on the floor to drink it and study her sketches. It was quieter now. The wind had dropped, the shutters had stopped rattling and there was only an occasional scrape of a branch against the outside wall. It was cooler, getting cold, and when she first caught the sound below of creaking boards she decided the old wood of the plank floor was contracting from the chill. But she raised her head and listened, looking toward the open door and the black hall and stairway.

Those could be footsteps. It could be someone moving slowly inside the large hall. No, it couldn't, dammit. It was only her tense nerves, her imagination. . . . She froze when she heard a thump against something solid, an indrawn breath, then silence.

Someone was down there. Sam Ormond? He would have turned on the lights and called to her. It could be a bum looking for a place to sleep. A drug addict looking for something to steal. A rapist who knew she was there alone.

Shock flashed through her, icy cold. She opened her mouth to scream, then shut it again. What good would it do? There was no one to hear, not in this deserted place. *Sit still, very still. Maybe he'll go away....* Her eyes wide with terror, she searched the littered room, looking for something, anything, she could use to defend herself. Still she didn't move—she couldn't—not until she heard the first creaking step on the old staircase. Then suddenly she was deeply, furiously angry. Angry enough to burn away panic. After everything else, this was just too much. Dammit, hadn't she been hurt enough?

She had only one chance—take him by surprise. And there was only one place to do it. She drew a deep breath, jerked off her shoes and grabbed a hammer that lay by the wall. Trembling with rage, she slipped into the darkness of the hall, keeping to the side, away from the light. She crept to the staircase and peered down.

There. In the blackness a moving shape, coming around the landing. She heard the tap of shoes on the bare boards. She drew back, her heart thundering so, she thought the invader would surely hear it. Her muscles tensed, she held the hammer ready. He'd never know what hit him. He'd be blinded by the light from the open door.

Now? No. Fury and fear thrummed in her throat. *Wait, and be sure not to miss.* Another two steps. Gail gripped the balustrade and raised the hammer in her right hand, poised for a downward blow. Up another step and—the man turned his head toward the doorway, his tightly curled hair glinting bronze in the shaft of light.

"Gail? Are you up there?"

"Alec!" Her startled shriek echoed through the empty house; the heavy hammer dropped from her lifeless hand, struck Alec's shoulder a light, glancing blow and continued down the staircase with a clattering fury of its own. Gail dropped to the floor of the hall, covering her face with both hands. "Dear God," she whispered, choking, "I could have *killed* you."

Alec was up and around the balustrade, pulling her to her feet. "My fault, darling," he said, shaken. "All my fault. What a fool I was. Of course you were scared! I'm so *sorry*—"

The wind was knocked out of him as Gail flung herself against him, sobbing, burrowing her face in his neck. Her arms around his waist, she hugged him with all her strength and babbled between her sobs.

"G-going to h-hit him with that ha-hammer, try to knock him out...I would h-have *died* if I'd hurt you...." She felt herself moving into the lighted room, Alec's arms around her, urging her along.

"Shh now," he murmured, stroking her hair. "It's all right. No one is hurt." He kept on murmuring soothingly and stroking her hair. When she finally grew quieter he pushed his handkerchief into her hand. "It was my fault," he said again as she wiped her face. "Lena told me where you were, but I should have yelled as soon as I came in. I wasn't thinking about you hearing me down there.... Hell, I haven't been able to think, at all. I can't stand not seeing you, Gail."

Scarlet-faced from weeping, Gail turned back into his arms and held him again, infinitely grateful for the warm, hard-muscled body against her, the miracle of having him close. "I can't stand it, either," she said hopelessly. "I know it's right for us to stay apart, but it's killing me. I can't go along with your contract, but I can't handle the way I feel."

"I'll settle for anything that keeps us together," Alec said unsteadily. "Anything. Just come back to me."

Gail lifted her head and looked up at him. "The way we were? Just two people together because we want to be? No 'wherefore' or 'whereas'?"

"If that's what you want, then that's what we'll be."

She dropped her head to his shoulder and took a deep breath. Life seemed to flow in with the air, filling the empty spaces inside. How could she have thought of leaving him? Why had she thought she could?

"I'm back with you. Let's go home."

Alec followed her station wagon to her place and went in with her. When he turned on lights and looked at her, her eyes were so big, so intensely blue in her pale face. She appeared immensely fatigued, as though she hadn't slept much of late. He knew his own face was drawn, lined beneath the cheekbones, hollowed around his eyes. He hadn't been sleeping, either. Now he felt both incredibly grateful and shaky, like a man jerked back to firm ground from a crumbling precipice. Without her, the future had been an empty chasm yawning before him. He watched her put her notebook and drawing pad on a small table, her hands still trembling a little, and thought how close he had come to losing her.

"Gail..."

She straightened and turned, then was in his arms.

"Gail," he said again, trembling himself. He bent, tenderly touching her eyelids with his lips, closing out the look of love and need. Moving to her lips, he felt his own need shaking him, choking him, running like fire through his veins. He kissed her ravenously, holding her silky head between his hands, searching out each warm, wet corner of her softly opening mouth.

Breathing in his scent, Gail flowed against him, giving herself over to the hard, pressing angles of his body. She welcomed the questing hands that shaped the outside curves of her breasts, that ran down to cup her buttocks and pull her tight against him. Her own desire burst inside, flowering into a wonderful, aching heat that tilted her hips up to his swelling arousal and made her gasp with wanting more.

"Alec . . . oh, Alec, I want you so much. I want you now. Please . . ."

She was in his arms, cradled across his chest, being carried into her bedroom and put down gently on the bed. "Yes," he said hoarsely. "Yes! We need each other. We always will." Urgently, awkwardly, he began to undress her.

She was naked in a matter of moments and sitting up in the bed, her flood of dark red hair half obscuring her face as she worked industriously to remove his shirt.

"A tie," she said, and shook her head. "A tie clasp. A long-sleeved shirt with teeny little buttons. An undershirt. A belt. Heavy trousers and jockey shorts. Laced shoes and long socks." She had the belt off, the trousers unzipped, her slender hands moving inside and circling his lean hips, pushing cloth down. She smiled up at him, her eyes a burning blue. "I should think that by the time you got all those things off you'd be out of the notion."

"I'm not."

She laughed, a throaty, warm sound of amusement, and touched him intimately. "I noticed."

Clothes still dangling in several stages of undress, he tipped her backward on the bed and went down with her, laughing unsteadily. "Be careful, angel. I may not be responsible for..." He gasped as she arched beneath him, guiding him inside, wrapping her legs around his thighs. "Oh, darling...my sweet darling."

She felt his powerful thrust, the thick, hot joining of their bodies, the muscles rolling on his smooth-skinned back, and all the problems between them fell away. There was only this, only the ecstasy, the closeness, the pure brilliance of sensation. Everything else would fall into place.

WHEN HE FOUND TIME to look at it, Alec was fascinated by Gail's small bedroom. Lying with her in the narrow bed, his body relaxed and glowing with utter satisfaction, he let his eyes wander over the ruffled curtains, the framed photograph of her parents on the chest of drawers, the little dressing table with its triple mirror, then to the foot of the delicate four-poster bed, where his own feet peeked out from beneath a luxurious, down-filled, satin-covered comforter. He smiled faintly. The room was like her. Neat, feminine and family oriented, but with a wide sensuous streak, soft and satiny. Lord, but he was lucky.

His gaze came back to Gail's sleeping face, the soft lips slightly parted, the thick lashes against her cheeks. He could see the gentle rise and fall of her breasts under the covers, and his hand, resting on her narrow waist, moved up involuntarily to cup one, to feel the round, firm warmth. In a moment his body reacted again, and he swelled against her silky thigh. He sighed inaudibly and buried his face in the tangle of dark red, fragrant hair on the pillow. They had made love twice earlier, and he couldn't wake her now. She needed this sleep.

In a moment her breathing altered, and rather than waking her, he pulled away, sliding restlessly from the bed. Time someone turned out that little light, anyway, he thought, and went to the dressing table to switch it off. Then he padded to the partially open window and let the cold drift of air cool his heated body.

Standing there, he wondered where he had failed. Nothing seemed to be working out as he had planned. He had wanted a wife he could control, but nothing he'd offered Gail seemed to tempt her. He simply couldn't believe how she was asking for nothing, giving him so much.

A splatter of heavy raindrops hit the window; the wind was rising again, gusting and colder. Alec shivered and turned back toward the bed, trying to be quiet, easing in. Gail rolled onto her side and yawned, opening her arms and taking him in, her warm hands running over his chilled flesh.

"Crazy man," she whispered drowsily. "You're freezing. Let me warm you." She pulled the comforter up to his ears, and beneath it her hands began long, luxuriously slow strokes. Alec groaned and pulled her closer. But just before desire blotted out the world, he wondered uneasily if under her warmth and caring hid a more subtle desire . . . to control *him.*

IN A DAY they had fallen back into the pattern they had been in before that disastrous evening of the premarital agreement—always together except when they worked, and carelessly happy. When Gail insisted on keeping the promise she'd made to Sam Ormond, Alec went with her the two more nights it took to finish her preliminary work.

He helped, his extra height and long arms useful in the job of measuring for draperies.

"When I advertise for an assistant," Gail said, writing down the measurements, "I'm going to say that no one under six feet need apply." She looked up from her seat on the floor with an impish grin. "Basketball players will be given a bonus."

"Female basketball players will be given a bonus," Alec said. "Males will be given a punch in the nose. I don't want my woman trailing around with another man."

"Hmm." Gail went on writing, her eyes on her notebook. "It seems to me I've seen two very attractive nurses going in and out of your offices, Doctor."

Alec grinned. "Are you jealous?" he asked, teasing. "Tell me you're jealous, Gail."

She looked up and laughed at him. "No, and neither are you. You aren't the kind to be unfaithful. And neither am I. You're all the man I'll ever need, darling. My one and only."

She was sitting cross-legged on the dusty floor, wearing old jeans and a turtleneck, a flannel shirt of his draped over her shoulders to ward off the chill in the old house. Staring down at her, Alec took in the amused blue eyes, the red hair shining in the harsh light of an overhead bulb and wished fervently that he could believe every word.

"Then why not marry me?" he blurted out. "*I'd* never leave *you*."

Gail's smile died. It was so plain what he meant. He would be faithful, but she couldn't be trusted. That was the whole reason for that damnable agreement, just as she'd thought from the beginning. She folded her notebook and stood, brushing the dust from her jeans.

"When you love me enough to trust me," she said quietly, "ask me again."

Alec made a gruff sound in his chest and swung away. "If you wanted me badly enough," he said, "you'd sign that agreement. You just don't want to be fenced in by some of the terms." His gaze, coming back to her, was cool and cynical. "Don't you think I can see that, Gail? Anyone could. If you were absolutely sure you'd never want out, you'd sign it in a minute."

"I would not." Her chin rose; her look was challenging. "I have no doubts about how I feel. It's the way you feel that worries me. And you'll have to figure that out for yourself. In the meantime, let's drop the subject. It makes both of us miserable."

Alec growled, but he said no more. He told himself he was giving her time, yet he knew his real reason was simple fear that she'd drop him if he didn't. Lord, but she was stubborn. Going with her on the Ormond job had shown him how much effort and time she put into her work, for a third or less of the money he'd offered her just as a personal allowance.

Thinking about it just before dawn, after he'd walked her back to her place, Alec decided it didn't make sense—unless she had reasons of her own. She must know how much he wanted her. Was she taking the chance that eventually he'd give in and marry her without the agreement? Was she making sure that if she tired of him, she could leave with a fat settlement?

The idea that Gail could be so conniving left a sick feeling in his stomach. But women *were* conniving. If he'd learned anything from his marriage to Marian, he'd learned that. No, he'd stick to his guns. No contract, no marriage. And maybe he'd do a little conniving himself. If Gail wasn't so damn sure of him, maybe she'd change her mind. It was worth a try.

AT DAWN, bundled in a thick navy pea coat and a bright yellow scarf, Gail walked along the seawall with Puppy, lately rescued from being spoiled by Virginia. A cold north wind and spitting rain had discouraged most of the joggers, but she was still surprised not to see Alec. He never missed. The thought crossed her mind that he might not be feeling well, and later, dressing for work, she called him to find out.

"I'm fine," Alec said when she asked. "It just wasn't much of a morning for running."

"Oh." He sounded, Gail thought, remote and disinterested. She frowned, puzzled. "Yes, it was rather nasty as mornings go. Glad you're all right. See you later then."

"Wait." Alec hesitated a moment, then went on rapidly. "I meant to tell you last night that I wouldn't be seeing you this evening. There's a . . . medical meeting I have to attend. You don't mind, do you? It could last a good part of the night."

"I don't mind at all," Gail assured him. "I can use the time myself to catch up on a few things I've neglected." She laughed a little. "I've let too much slide lately—and I'll bet you have, too. Give me a call when you're free."

Hanging up, Alec felt a sour disappointment. He couldn't make up his mind if Gail had sounded simply cheerful or a bit relieved. Neither tone suited him. Neither did going to the medical meeting, which was only the routine, monthly session of the hospital board. Tilting back his chair, he glanced at his desk calendar.

November 15. He had now been with Gail more than two months—nearly two and a half—and if anything, he was farther away from what he wanted than he had been the first week. He had begun to think it would take a miracle to convince her they should be married.

The phone beside him rang, surprising him. Penny didn't often put through calls before ten. Slightly irritated, he picked it up.

"Yes?"

"This is someone I think you'll be glad to hear from," Penny said. "Let me put him on."

"Dad?" The clear young voice was breaking with excitement. "Can you come get me?"

Alec's tilted chair came down with a crash. "Bru! Where are you?"

"I'm here!" Bru's laugh was shaky. "I mean, I'm in Florida. Some place called Jeffersonville, I think. I saved up my allowance for a ticket and left that dumb school. Wait a minute—"

Alec gripped the phone, listening to a mumble of questions and answers. Jeffersonville? Where was he? Oh, Lord, if he got cut off....

"It's Jacksonville," Bru said at last. "It's supposed to be close to St. Augustine. I'm in the airport. Can you come soon? I'm hungry."

Alec closed his eyes and groaned. "I'm leaving now, Bru. It'll take some time, but don't you dare leave the building. Don't talk to anybody. Sit down in a chair and wait for me. Promise?"

"I promise," Bru said, subdued. "You mad at me?"

"No. But I will be if you move an inch!" Alec roared. He slammed down the phone and raced from his office, through the waiting room and out the front door, heading south. Ahead of him he saw Gail pulling out of the driveway, stopping to let a car pass.

"Gail!"

Startled, she stared at him as he ran up and jerked open the car door.

"I need you," he managed breathlessly. "Will you help me?"

"Of course," Gail said instantly. "How?"

"Bru ran away. He's in an airport in Jacksonville, alone. I've no idea where the damn airport *is*! I've never been in Jacksonville. If you'll come with me..."

Gail gasped. "Good Lord! Get in! Don't waste time getting your car. I'll take you there."

They were on the highway and speeding north before Alec spoke again, gruffly.

"I'm sorry. This is stupid, taking your time. Anyone in Jacksonville could have told me where to go. I guess I lost my head."

Gail took a quick look at him. Body taut as a bowstring, hands clenched on his thighs, the expression in his usually cynical eyes painfully vulnerable. Love and sympathy tightened her throat.

"I'm glad you asked me. You'd have wasted an hour going clear into Jacksonville and getting directions. A little boy gets restless waiting."

Alec nodded, eyes fixed on the road. "He's hungry, too," he added abruptly. "He said so."

Gail smiled, weaving in and out of slower-moving traffic. "That won't hurt him. They always are at that age." Settling back into the right lane, she glanced over at him again. "He'll be all right, Alec."

Alec nodded, straightening in the seat and trying to relax. "I suppose I should have expected this. Marian said she was putting him in a new school, and it's just like him to figure a way out. That's the trouble with having kids. They can scare the hell out of you."

Gail laughed softly. "True. But, to coin an old saw, that comes with the territory. It's worth it, isn't it?"

"Yes," Alec said, letting his breath out. "But wait until I get my hands on him. His mother is probably frantic."

Gail's brows rose. If so, she thought, accelerating to pass a sputtering old truck, why hadn't *she* called to let Alec know, to ask for help, to find out if their son had come to Florida. Surely the school would have let her know he was missing.

8

BRUCE MORGAN would have been easy to find, Gail thought, even if she'd come after him alone. The tight bronze curls on his head shone like a beacon under the lights in the waiting room. Long-legged and slender, in the usual T-shirt and jeans, Bru was sitting between two bored-looking teenagers. Suddenly he leaped up and ran, awkwardly dodging back and forth in the crowd, to fling himself at Alec.

"Dad!" His arms around Alec's waist, Bru pushed his face into his father's shirt, his chest heaving as he fought tears.

Alec picked him up, his face contorted. "Listen here, young man," he began, then laughed unevenly and hugged him hard. "All right, you're here," he said, putting him down. "Now let's call your mother and tell her you're okay."

Bru swiped at his face with one hand and clung to Alec's belt with the other. "We can't," he said matter-of-factly. "She isn't home." He stared up at Gail with damp green eyes, his grin fading. "Who're you?"

Gail smiled. She recognized immediately that he had hoped to have his dad to himself, and didn't blame him a bit. "I'm Gail, one of your father's friends. If you can't call your mother, how about calling your school?"

Bru frowned and shook his head. "I don't want to go back." He turned and looked at Alec. "That new school is lousy, Dad. Can't I stay here with you?"

"We'll see. Where's your mother?"

"In France, I think." Bru was rapidly regaining a careless, nine-year-old composure. "She and ol' Roger are on a trip. She calls me sometimes, but I haven't seen her in a couple of months."

Alec exploded. "Two months? She said two weeks!" They were standing like an island in an eddying stream of arriving and departing passengers, who turned to stare when Alec raised his voice. He glared at them, reddening, then grabbed Gail's arm and Bru's hand and started toward the door. "Never mind," he growled. "We'll talk in the car."

"Wait. First things first," Gail said, halting his long stride. "As I recall, the hamburgers here are great. Hungry, Bru?"

Bru glanced up suspiciously, then focused on the floor. "I sure am. I haven't had anything to eat but a chocolate bar since I left."

Alec groaned. "I forgot. Where, Gail?"

Gail waved a hand. "Over there, past the souvenir shop. Any luggage, Bru? I'll go get it."

He gave her a blank look. "I didn't bring any. Someone would've seen the suitcase and stopped me. Anyway, I didn't have any other jeans and I sure didn't want those dumb school uniforms."

"Right," Gail said calmly. "Let's eat."

A cup of coffee later, Alec had simmered down. "I don't understand," he said to Bru, "how you managed to leave a private school and get on a plane by yourself. Didn't anyone see you leave the grounds or ask any questions when you went for a ticket?"

"There's this guy, Jim," Bru said, flooding his second hamburger with ketchup, "who mows the grass at school. He's old—he's almost twenty. He has this truck he carries his mower in, and we made a deal. First I hid in the truck, then he took me to the airport and got me a ticket and I gave him my stereo." He looked up at Alec. "He's a nice guy, Dad. He told the stewardess to look after me. He said he'd get fired if anyone at the school heard he helped me. You won't tell, will you?"

"I'll have to think about that," Alec said shortly. "Which reminds me, I'd better call now. Tell me the principal's name, son."

Bru looked up, his jaw stiffening in a remarkably familiar way. "No."

Gail sighed, watching as Alec and his son glared at each other across the table, their expressions identical.

"Don't be rude," Alec said. "You know you will."

"I'll say I did it alone," Bru said stubbornly. "In fact, I did, really. It was *my* idea. I talked him into it."

Gail looked from one to the other and grinned. "It can wait until you get home," she said.

"FROM WHAT BRU SAYS," Alec remarked the next day, "this new school is more of a boarding home for the children of the wealthy. Strict security—that's a laugh—and easy classes. Tutors if the parents want them badly enough to pay. A lot of luxury. Most of the children are under ten."

It was noon, and they were sitting in Gail's kitchen with the back door open, watching Bru toss sticks for Puppy in the walled yard. Gail frowned at the description Alec gave.

"Baby-sitting with frills?"

Alec nodded. "Bru's been there since the middle of August."

"That long? *Why?*"

"It seems that's when Marian left for Europe," Alec said, frowning. "But Bru didn't mind that. He said it was better at first than staying at home, because he had other kids to play with." He glanced at Gail, then looked away again. "The Hewlett house is a show-place. Not much room for playing."

"Does Marian—" Gail paused, the name strange on her tongue. "Does Bru's mother want you to send him right back?"

"So far," Alec said evenly, "she doesn't know he left. She's supposed to leave a number and information about where she is, but the school hasn't been able to get in touch with her. Anyway, the principal was glad to know Bru's safe, but he doesn't want him back. He says Bru's a rebel."

Gail smiled. "You didn't tell on the yardman, I hope."

Alec grinned for the first time in two days. "You're worse than Bru. No, I didn't tell—I couldn't. Bru held out for that promise."

"I thought he would," Gail said. "He's a good kid. You're going to keep him here, then?"

"As long as I can." He met Gail's eyes. "I wish I had that country house built and you in it. I'd do my best to get Marian to agree to let me have him full-time. As it is, Penny watches over him like a grandmother. He loves it."

Gail laughed, purposely ignoring the remark about the country house and her in it. "Milk and cookies and bedtime stories?"

"How did you know?"

"An educated guess. I baby-sat for spending money in high school. I enticed a lot of little boys into bed with snacks and stories."

"Hmm. You've never offered me snacks and stories."

Gail chuckled. "I've never needed to. But if you feel deprived, you can ask for what you want."

"That doesn't seem to work, either," Alec said wryly. "I ask and ask for what I want and all you say is no." He got up and went to the back door to call Bruce.

"Time to go, Bru. Gail and I have to work this afternoon." He turned back to Gail with his ironic smile. "I suppose the chance of your saying yes is even slimmer, now that you might have to take on my son, too."

A flash of anger heated in Gail's cheeks. "Don't be so damnably bitter, Alec. What kind of a person do you think I am? Do you really believe I'd resent having a boy like Bru?"

Bursting through the open back door together, Bru and Puppy put an end to the quarrel. Bru skidded to a stop by Gail's chair, giving her a challenging glance.

"You know what, Gail? This killer dog of yours *likes* me."

Gail managed a smile. "Of course he does. He knows the good guys from the bad guys."

At the moment, Puppy was leaning against Alec's thigh, looking up soulfully and wagging his tail. Alec gave Gail a rueful look.

"He likes me, too. Do you still trust his judgment?"

Gail had to laugh. "I'm willing to grant that you're one of the good guys," she said. "But maybe a little mixed up."

"I bet you'd like Dad even if your dog didn't," Bru said jealously, looking back as he and Alec left. "Everybody else does."

Alec caught her glance and grinned. "I hired him to say that. Don't forget—Pizza Palace tomorrow for lunch."

"I'll remember." Watching them leave, Alec's hand casually rested on Bru's shoulder, Bru's fingers hooked as usual in the back of Alec's belt, she thought how much closer they were than most modern fathers and sons. As they reached the sidewalk and turned north, she saw Bru's face turn up with a laugh at something Alec had said. Even from the door she could see the adoration in the boy's face.

Back in the kitchen, Gail put the Dobie out in the yard and hurried through the few dishes from the lunch she had made for them. Bru was so happy to be with his father—but how long could it last? Someday there'd be a call and he'd be on his way north again. She was still thinking about him as she left for her afternoon appointment. If only . . . but no mother would give up Bru.

RESTLESS THAT NIGHT when he arrived at her house, Alec suggested a walk. The dark air was clear and cold, but windless; only a faint drift of breeze came from the sea and across Mantanzas Bay. They walked along the brightly lighted seawall to the end near the fort, then stopped, leaning on the rough stone to talk about Bru, now fast asleep in the loft, with Penny on guard, knitting in the big room below.

"There's not much for him to do around here," Alec said soberly, "but it would be silly to put him in school unless Marian leaves him here through the holidays. Even then it would only be the month between Thanksgiving and Christmas."

Gail stared out at the dark water. She knew what she wanted to suggest, but she thought she'd give it a little more thought. She changed the subject.

"Speaking of Thanksgiving," she said, "my mother has invited all three of us to dinner. She called just before you came over and when I told her about Bru she insisted on having us. You know how she is about children. Of course, if you'd rather not, then I'll tell her you've made other plans."

Alec laughed. "You know I never refuse your mother's cooking, and as for Bru I can't think of anything better. He's never been to a Thanksgiving dinner."

Gail stared at him, puzzled. "You mean except at home."

"I mean anywhere. Marian didn't bother with Thanksgiving. She prefers more sophisticated parties."

"Oh." Recovering, Gail laughed. "Then you'd better spend tomorrow filling Bru in on the Pilgrims and Indians and turkeys. In the meantime, let's go home. I'm cold."

Alec grinned and put an arm around her, and they headed for Charlotte Street. "That's not true," he said. "You're stubborn and full of illusions, but you're not cold. You're beautifully warm, angel. Including your heart. You've handled Bru just right—he was jealous of sharing his dad at first, but you're winning him over fast."

She snuggled closer, putting her arm around his waist. He was different; his bitterness was gone and there was a look of happiness in his eyes. Having his son again changed him completely. "I've got a secret weapon," she said, smiling, "Puppy, the Killer Dog."

ALEC'S USUALLY NEAT living quarters were cluttered with opened packages and strewn with new T-shirts and jeans, socks and underwear, bought in a hurry that morning before Alec's office hours. Once Penny had gathered up her knitting and said good-night, Gail began picking them up.

"You've achieved that lived-in look at last," she told Alec, folding shirts into a neat pile. "Where should I put these?"

"Down," Alec said. "I didn't bring you here to clean up after a nine-year-old." He took the shirts from her, tossed them on the couch and pulled her into his arms. The heat of his body enveloped her; the urgency of his kiss jolted her into an instant response. Softly his tongue asked, then demanded surrender; his hands slipped within her coat and slid down her back, cupping her buttocks and pressing her tightly into the cradle of his thighs.

"I still need you," he whispered in her ear. "I've found out I'm always going to need you. Bru's here and he's safe. Let's think about us."

The magic was there. It was always there, waiting to be wakened. Gail's fingers threaded through his bright hair and held him while she returned his kiss, teasing his broad mouth with flicks of her tongue. Fitting herself to his long body, she tilted her lips and moved slowly and sensuously against his loins. "Now," she breathed, "are you thinking of us?"

"Lovely witch," Alec gasped, "who's thinking?" His mouth fastened on hers again; his hands rose to her shoulders and pushed her coat down. Dropping her hands, Gail let the coat fall. In minutes there was a new trail of strewn clothes, leading into the bedroom.

Tossed like a leaf on the brilliant blue throw, Gail drew in her breath as Alec flung himself down beside her and pulled her into his arms. He was never the same; there was no pattern to his moody lovemaking, sometimes slow and gentle, sometimes stormy with passion, other times funny and sweet, making her laugh. Tonight the storm signals were flying. . . .

Leaning over her, entangling both hands in her thick hair, Alec stared down into her darkening eyes. "You *belong* to me," he said gruffly. "All of you. You're my woman." He bent, his mouth opening wide to suck in as much as he could of a breast, the tight nipple, the white flesh around the dark rose aureole. His rough tongue licked and tugged until she gasped and arched with pleasure. "Hold still," he growled, mock angry, and trailed his open mouth across the soft, deep valley to take the other one. "This is *my* night."

Quivering, feeling the exquisite pain of desire flooding through her veins, Gail stroked the soft tumble of his hair and held him close. Maybe tonight he needed to believe she was all his. Maybe tonight she was.

She yielded completely as he began to move over her breathless body, branding every inch with his exploring hand, the hot seal of his mouth. She could feel his deep excitement, the building strength of his passion, and somewhere inside, an ancient female instinct exulted. She *wanted* to be taken by storm, to know the ultimate surrender of her body to his. To be one with him.

The night was so still. Not a whisper of a leaf stirred the air. The only sounds were the sounds they made, quick little sighs, labored breathing. All her senses were acute, her skin keenly aware of the slightest touch, of the woolly softness of the blue throw beneath her, of the heat of his breath on her thighs, the velvet of his tongue on her most sensitive spot. The sounds she heard then came from her own throat, husky and pleading.

Alec twisted lithely and covered her, a soft, answering growl in his chest. He took her with a deep kiss and a long, slow thrust; then, tossing control to the winds, he swept her into the plunging storm of desire that possessed him.

Later, reaching a long arm for the edge of the woolly throw, Alec pulled it over their cooling bodies, wrapping it close, encasing them together in a blue cocoon.

"Don't go home," he said drowsily. "Stay with me."

"You know I can't."

He turned a little, his intent eyes scanning her sleepy but stubborn face. "Won't, you mean."

Gail blinked, surprised, then lifted a shoulder in a half shrug. "Whatever."

Alec smiled, kissed the shoulder, then her eyes, shutting the drooping lids. "You really don't belong to me, do you, angel?"

She yawned and opened her eyes. "In so far as I am able to belong to anyone except myself," she said with drowsy dignity, "I belong to you. Mainly because I love you."

Alec's breath caught in his throat; his lax arms tightened and drew her close. "Illusion becomes you," he said unevenly. "I hope you never lose it."

Gail drew back and looked at him. "Illusion? Is the way you feel about Bru an illusion?"

"Bru's my son," Alec said, reddening. "That's different."

"Of course it is. But it's still love."

"I suppose you could say that," Alec admitted cautiously, and threw back the covers. It sounded like an argument he couldn't win. He slid from the bed and went to get her clothes from the living room, disgusted with himself. He should never have mentioned illusions. But he hadn't been thinking. He'd reacted like a starry-eyed kid when she'd said she loved him.

Coming back into the bedroom, he saw she was up, standing and looking at the print of the storm, her naked body outlined by the light from the little lamp. He hesitated, caught by her delicacy and grace. The gleaming light slanted across her high breasts as she turned and smiled at him.

"The first time I saw this print," she said, "I remember thinking that it was too turbulent for the bedroom. I was wrong. It suits you."

Alec dropped her clothes on the bed and went to her, fascinated by the play of light and shadow on her ivory skin, the gleaming curves and dark hollows. "Is that what you think I am?" he asked, drawing her to him. "Too turbulent?"

She laughed and kissed him. "You have your stormy nights, lover. But I'm not objecting—I'm stronger than I look, and I love it. Let me dress now. It's very late."

He let her go and picked up his own clothes. She *was* strong, maybe too strong in some ways. Not a good choice for a man who wanted a wife he could manage. He would have been better off, he thought, with a more submissive woman. Tying his shoes, he wondered, briefly, how it would be with someone else, someone who would bend to his wishes. Straightening, he glanced over at Gail, dressed again, standing at the mirror and brushing her hair. She caught his glance in the mirror and smiled at him, her eyes soft. Jolted, he turned away. He didn't have a choice. He couldn't imagine giving her up.

DRIVING OUT to the Winslows' house on Thanksgiving, Bru sat in the back seat with Puppy, contented and mostly quiet.

"Puppy is a dumb name for a killer dog," he volunteered. "I think I'll call him Slash."

Gail hushed him. "You'll hurt his feelings," she said lightly. "He likes his name."

"He might like Slash better."

"You can try it," Gail said generously. "When we get there you can take him out in the fields and call him by that name. If he comes, he likes it."

Alec grinned, slanting a glance at her. "You're taking a chance there, angel."

She laughed and then shrugged. They both knew how the Dobie was with Bru, following him constantly, alert to every word. "So, if I have to, I'll call him Slash."

"Great name," Bru said enthusiastically. "How'd you ever think of it?" He fell back in the seat, laughing and fondling Puppy's ears. "Puppy, I now pronounce you Slash. Don't you dare forget it."

The Dobie yawned and lay down across Bru's skinny legs like an oversize lap dog. Catching the action in the rearview mirror, Alec laughed.

"I wish I had Bru's powers of persuasion. He gets around both of you."

I wish I had Bru, Gail thought, and was silent with surprise. Was she doomed always to want what she couldn't have?

9

FOR ONCE Virginia Winslow didn't dash out to greet them as they drove up.

"They're both in the kitchen," Gail guessed aloud, and opened the door. Puppy squeezed out to gallop for the trees, but Gail grabbed the back of Bru's shirt as he tried to follow. "First you come in and meet my parents," she said firmly. "Then you can go out and call Puppy."

Bru gave her a surprised look, but he didn't struggle. "Slash," he reminded her, tucking in his shirt again. "Hey, look at all the *woods* around here! Can I go exploring?"

"I'll show you the limits," Alec said, coming around the car. "After you've been introduced to the Winslows. Remember your manners."

David Winslow met them as they entered; he was coming from the kitchen, drying his hands. He stared down at Bru, a slow, delighted smile crinkling his eyes, then shook hands with him.

"So you've come to have Thanksgiving dinner with us."

"Yes, sir. Did you ask any Indians?"

Dave laughed. "I'm afraid not. It's just us Pilgrims. But maybe we can fix that."

"Darlings, you're here!" caroled Virginia, hurrying out to join them. "And this is *Bru!*" She stopped and stared at him. Green eyes met green eyes and both Virginia and Bru smiled. "You're exactly the way I thought you'd be," Virginia said, hugging him. "You look just like your father."

Bru gave her his sudden grin. "You smell like chocolate chip cookies, Mrs. Winslow."

"Call me 'Grandma,' and I'll give you a handful."

Five minutes later Alec, Dave and Bru, fortified with cookies, left by the back door to set limits and, according to Bru, to find Slash.

"Slash?" Virginia asked wonderingly, looking at Gail. "Who or what is Slash?"

Standing at the back door, Gail pointed. "That large black killer dog running toward Bru."

"Don't be silly," Virginia said.

"But Puppy is a dumb name for a killer dog."

"Oh." Getting it, Virginia laughed, then sobered as she looked at Gail consideringly. "You really like Bru, don't you?"

"I do," Gail said, turning toward the stove. "But I don't want to talk about it. Let's finish up this dinner. The turkey smells delicious."

Alec came back in time to carry in to the laden table the silver platter holding a huge, golden-brown turkey. "They'll be along in a minute," he said in answer to Virginia's questioning look about Dave and Bru. "Dave's fixing up Bru in his workshop." He grinned at Gail. "Slash is with them."

Bru arrived wearing a fitted leather strap around his bright curls, decorated with several feathers. "Grandpa Dave said we needed a token Indian," he told Gail, looking pleased with himself. "And I'm it. These are *hawk* feathers. We found them in the woods. Did you know hawks have eyes like telescopes? They can see forever. Is all that food just for *us*?"

Gail nodded and smiled and watched her parents watch Bru all through the long dinner. Frustrated grandparents, mesmerized by one small boy, she thought. But, then, Bru was Bru—impossible to resist. He ate hugely and endeared himself even more to Virginia by asking for a second plate of pie.

"For me," he said, grinning. "The Indian ate the other one."

Virginia was unnaturally silent as she and Gail cleared the table and started on the dishes. Bru had gone to the den with Alec and Dave to watch football on TV. His whoop of triumph as someone scored resounded through the house.

"That's a perfectly lovely little boy," Virginia burst out. "Why don't you marry Alec and keep him?"

Gail shot her mother a sardonic look. "The world isn't going to rearrange itself just to give you a grandchild."

"I know," Virginia admitted. "But doesn't it break your heart to see how happy he is here, then to think of him having to go back? If you and Alec were married, a judge might—"

"Mother!"

"All right," Virginia muttered. "It's none of my business. But he's worth it. If I could keep him, I would."

Turning on the dishwasher, she looked back at Gail defiantly. "In fact, I'm going to ask Alec if we can have Bru out here with us during the day. Both of you work, and there's nothing for a boy to do in town. He'll have the whole outdoors to play in, and Dave would love having him around."

Gail laughed. "And so would you. Go ahead and ask. It would be good for Bru, I admit, and he could bring Puppy along."

"Slash," Virginia corrected.

THEY LEFT in late afternoon. Virginia followed them out onto the steps, waited until Bru was busy settling the Dobie in the car and then asked. Alec frowned.

"Sure you want to, Ginny? A nine-year-old can be a handful."

"I'm sure. We need some young blood around here, don't we, David?"

Dave grinned. "Leave him now if you want to."

Alec laughed. "Thanks, but, no. I like to be with him as much as I can. I'll ask him, Ginny. If he wants to come, though, I'll do the driving, not you. I'll be wanting to check on the house, anyway."

Gail gave him a startled glance. "House?"

"Didn't I tell you?" Alec asked smoothly. "The foundation goes in tomorrow."

"You're building?" Dave asked, surprised. "Where?"

"Why, on the land I bought south of here. I thought Gail told you—we'll be neighbors, Dave."

"Well, that's great news," Dave said, puzzled but pleased.

But Virginia looked daggers at Gail. "Our daughter," she said acidly, "never tells us anything."

"It was none of my business," Gail said desperately, and Alec smiled, taking her arm.

"Your daughter," he said lightly, "has a hard time making up her mind. When she does, I'm hoping she'll marry me and live in that house."

Speechless, Gail went with him to the car. "I could kill you," she muttered as they drove away. "You *promised* me you wouldn't say anything to them."

"I don't see why you're so angry," Alec said, "they looked rather pleased."

"Shocked," Gail said, between clenched teeth.

"That, too," Alec admitted, and grinned. "It had to come out sometime, angel."

"What are you guys talking about?" Bru asked, interested. "Did Dad spill a secret, Gail?"

Gail looked around at Bru's wide eyes and pushed down her anger. "Your dad just likes to kid around, Bru. Sometimes he makes me mad."

Bru laughed. "He teases me, too, Gail. But he doesn't mean it."

There was that to consider, as well, Gail thought. Alec had sounded only half-serious. But she wished he hadn't mentioned even the possibility in front of her parents—Virginia would order a wedding gown. Gail felt his gaze on her and looked over, catching a small, apologetic smile.

"It's going to be a wonderful house, Gail."

"I'm sure it is," she said generously. "And Bru will love being out here in the woods. I'm really glad you're building it."

"I hope he will," Alec said, grinning and checking the rearview mirror. "Maybe I'll find a lady who can make chocolate chip cookies. You'd really like that, Bru. You'd have a family again."

"I guess so," Bru said slowly, "but...I like us the way we are."

"You deserved that," Gail said, staring at the bottom of her empty coffee cup. "You can't just run roughshod over other people. You have to remember that family life didn't suit Bru."

Lounging in a kitchen chair across from her, Alec shrugged. "I suppose it wasn't the right word. He equates family life with being mostly ignored. But he'll change his mind."

Gail frowned. Bru had been bedded down and Penny was on guard, she and Alec were alone in her kitchen, and she still couldn't think of the words she needed to explain everything she felt. It wasn't just Bru. She wasn't really worried about Bru. If everything else was right, she was sure they would get along. But . . .

"Do you think it was fair to pressure me by bringing my parents into this argument?"

"No."

She looked up at him, pushing her hair back from her face with a tired gesture. "Then why did you do it?"

"Desperation. I'd feel like an idiot moving into that house alone."

"I don't think that's funny, Alec."

He stood swiftly and took the cup from her hand, then lifted her from her chair, grasping her arms and looking into her eyes. All the put-on amusement was gone from his dark face.

"I know it isn't funny, dammit. I *am* desperate. You say you care for me—and you certainly act as if you do—but you won't give an inch! Let's go over that agreement together, and you tell me exactly what you want changed."

Gail's chin went up. "I'm not interested in the terms of that agreement, Alec. I'm interested in why you think it's necessary."

"Let's just say I've had experience," he replied harshly.

"So have I."

He dropped his hands from her arms and turned away. "For heaven's sake, Gail, don't be so naive. What experience? Two or three years of playing house in your early twenties? You have no idea of what can happen in the long run. People can change."

"Then you change," Gail said adamantly. "I certainly won't. If I get married it'll be by a minister, not a lawyer. And it'll be to a man who fulfills *my* requirements."

He swung around angrily. "Your fuzzy-headed illusions, you mean. I offered to change the agreement, and I meant it. In fact, after reading it over, I've decided myself that the provisions for you in case of divorce are really not fair. I'm willing to rewrite that part to include a decent alimony—"

"Shut up!" Gail interrupted, tears in her eyes. "Just shut up! Go home before I lose my temper completely. Dammit, Alec, I'm *not* Marian!"

The anger faded from Alec's eyes. "I'm sorry," he said finally. "Of course you're not. And I did promise not to bring up the agreement again." His wide mouth twisted in his familiar, ironic smile. "I'll leave. I don't blame you for kicking me out."

Gail followed him through the hall and into the living room, the Dobie close at her heels. *It's over*, she thought, and a wave of intense pain swept her. She set her jaw, reminding herself that it was inevitable. They were too far apart in their beliefs, and neither of them was going to give. She moved forward hesitantly, ready to lock the door when he left.

"I'm sorry it had to end this way," she said unevenly. "But I wish you well, Alec."

He turned, startled. "What are you talking about? Nothing is ending here but our latest quarrel."

"No, it's more than that—"

Sweeping her into his arms, he held her tightly. "You think I'll give you up? I'll never do that, Gail. You're in my life to stay, married or not." He pulled back and looked at her searchingly. "Do *you* want out?"

She shook her head, tears glistening on her lashes. "No, Alec." Her mouth tilted into a wry smile. "I know I should want out. I should be running now for the nearest exit. I guess I'm stubborn about that, too."

Alec kissed the corners of her mouth, the tear stains on her cheeks, then moved back to her waiting lips. "I think," he said a moment later, "that my mood's improving. In fact, I feel wonderful. And so do you, at least to me. Mind if I stay awhile?"

"No," Gail said faintly. "I don't mind a bit."

FOR THE NEXT FEW DAYS they carefully avoided any talk of the future, at least of their own futures. Alec had put aside his doubts and enrolled Bru in public school, and had made arrangements for him to be bused to the Winslows in the afternoons. Each day he picked him up and brought him home, tired and happy, to eat prodigiously and to go to bed.

"He looks great," Alec told Gail. "And he thinks public school is heaven. I hate to think of this ending."

Every day without a call was a bonus, Gail thought. One more happy day for Bru, one more for Alec and one more for her parents, who were convinced they had found the perfect boy for a grandson. As for her, she tried hard not to become too close to Bru, to treat him only as a casual young friend. She left Puppy at her parents' house for Bru, but that was all. He had, she thought, been very explicit about wanting to stay the way they were. It suited her own beliefs. She wasn't ready yet to give Alec up, but she felt forced to give up any thought of a future with him.

On Saturday, Alec kept Bru with him and the two of them spent the day exploring the fort, the tourist attractions, ending up over on Anastasia Island, swimming in a chilly sea.

"It was fun," Bru told Gail at dinner that evening. "But it would have been more fun if you'd gone with us. Why didn't you?"

"I had work to do," Gail said cheerfully. "Next time, maybe. Anyway, tomorrow we're all going out to the country together."

"Yeah! Dad and I'll take you to see the place where he's building a house. There's a lake there, and a lot of great big trees, a neat place for a camp and..." He went on, describing the glories, his eyes shining. Gail and Alec glanced at each other, then looked quickly away. Bru was so happy now, yet it couldn't last.

"I HAVE NEWS," Alec said the following Monday evening. "Marian called today."

Gail turned from the gleaming counter in Alec's kitchen and looked at him. Then she turned back and finished making the coffee he'd asked for, understanding why he had sent Bru up to his room early.

"I thought you seemed upset," she said. "Was she very angry?"

"No. She wasn't angry at all. She simply blamed the school for everything, including Simpson's 'failure' to let her know Bru was missing." Alec flung himself down at the polished walnut table and was silent as Gail found coffee mugs and brought them over. He was pale, his eyes tired. "I should have known she'd ease herself out of it," he added bitterly. "As far as she's concerned it was simply a childish lark. She laughed off any thought of Bru's being unhappy there."

Gail frowned and sat down with him. "Some lark. Did she say Bru had to come home right away?"

"No." Alec's mouth suddenly relaxed into a smile. "That's the good news. Due to the demands of a heavy social season in New York, she's going to wait until after the Christmas holidays to have someone care for him."

"That's great! But . . . who is this someone?"

Alec laughed shortly. "There's two of them. Louisa and Dick Sommers, her elder sister and her brother-in-law. She says they'll be in the Bahamas for December and will pick up Bru on the way home."

Gail frowned. "I see. But how will Bru feel about that? Maybe he'd rather have his mother come for him." She poured Alec a cup of coffee, then handed it to him and saw he was amused. "So?" she added, her frown deepening. "What's funny?"

"You are. Worrying about Bru while trying to pretend he's just another kid to you."

"I like him, Alec. I've never tried to hide that. Is he fond of the Sommers?"

Alec sighed. "I don't know. They weren't around much until Marian married Hewlett. I think they make themselves useful and hang on the fringes of the Hewlett money. They'll be over to make arrangements soon."

"That sounds all right," Gail said slowly. "But you don't look satisfied with it."

"I know. My problem is that I want to keep him here."

Gail hesitated, then blurted out, "Why not? Now that Bru has proved he wants to be with you, she might let you have him. Why don't you ask?"

Alec was silent as he gazed absently into his cup. "I did," he said at last. "I told her I had a place now and was building a house in the country, and that Bru wanted to stay." He pushed back his chair and sprang to his feet, beginning to pace. "She said no. I tried to point out that she'd be better off with more time for traveling and social life. I said she could see him whenever she wished and have him for a time in the summer, but she still said no." He stopped and swung to face Gail, his face hard. "She ended by saying a child his age was a bother, and I should be thankful to get out of having to keep him!"

Gail was swept by quick anger. "She sounds like a real winner, Alec. Couldn't you reason with her?"

"I tried. She just laughed it off."

"You have as much right as she does to—"

"The rights are equal," Alec shot back. "But custom is on the side of the mother. I found that out the hard way when we divorced."

She sat looking at him, knowing how hurt he was, how much he loved Bru and wanted him with him. "I wish I could help," she said softly. "I'd do anything I could."

Alec stood looking at her, his expression gradually softening. "I know you would, darling. But Marian hasn't done anything actionable, and she won't." He ran his fingers through his hair and managed a smile. "I'm dumping my problems all over you, and none of them are your fault. I'm sorry, Gail. Let's forget it."

"I didn't mind. Have you told Bru?"

"No," Alec said. "But of course I will. At least he'll have until the holidays are over. Let's make the best of it. We'll have a wonderful bang-up Christmas and New Year."

IN THE DAYS AHEAD Bru was too busy to be sad. He was thrilled by the freedom of public school and loved the noisy school bus; he went with Alec every afternoon to see the progress on the new house and planned his own room right down to the dog bed in a corner. He'd conveniently forgotten that the Dobie belonged to Gail, and now it seemed he refused to believe he would be going back north. Building impossible dreams, Gail thought, and her heart hurt for him. But there would be the summers, at least.

"TGIS," Alec said, opening the car door for Gail and grinning at her bemused expression. "Thank God It's Sunday," he explained, "and we'll be hidden in the country. No unwelcome visitors."

Gail laughed and let go of the Dobie's leash, allowing him to leap in the back with Bru. Alec had begun dreading the visit from the Sommers. Now, sliding in beside him, Gail thought how relieved he looked, how vibrant with happiness.

"A day off agrees with you," she teased.

"I'm beginning to hope," Alec said, putting the car in gear. Then he glanced warily into the rearview mirror at Bru's alert face. "You know what hope is, don't you? The irrepressible feeling that against all odds everything will come out just fine."

Gail laughed. "I'm all for that."

"So am I," Bru said, "if it means I get to stay here instead of having to go back."

Alec and Gail looked at each other, then away. No matter how they skirted the issue, how careful they were in what they said, Bru seemed to know what they were thinking. For the rest of the trip they talked about the new house, now framed and with a semblance of roof.

"The fast part is over," Alec said. "Now they begin the details. But it's time to show it to Gail, isn't it, Bru?"

"Yes! I'll show you where my room is, Gail. It's going to be super. I'll see the lake from my window. Did you know we have two technicolor ducks?"

"Wood ducks," Gail said absently.

"No, they're real. They fly and swim . . . stop laughing, Dad. You know they do."

Gail swallowed her own laughter. Every day Bru tunneled a tiny bit deeper into her heart. She knew now that she loved them both. Did it really matter that Alec didn't love her? He wanted her. He was kind. He'd be faithful; she was somehow sure of that. And they both loved Bru. Bru was still a little bit jealous, a little possessive about his dad, but he only needed to feel secure. She could see the three of them living in the country, close enough to her parents that Bru could be with them often. It would be an ideal life . . . but would it be enough?

"Dreaming, darling?"

She looked around, startled. There he was, and no, it wouldn't be enough. She would always want more than he could give. And that would always hurt her, and probably bore him. That divorce he kept talking about would become a real possibility. It took love from both sides to make a marriage.

"Yes," she said, "that's exactly what I was doing—dreaming."

10

THERE WAS A THICKET of silver-gray short-leaf pines on a sand ridge near the Winslow house and ten days before Christmas Dave took Bru along to help him pick out a tree.

"First" he told Bru solemnly "you watch for rattlesnakes. Then you look around for trees."

They brought back two trees, one for the Winslow living room and a small one for Alec's office.

"Next year," Bru said excitedly, "we'll have a great big one in our new house, Dad!" He turned and looked at Gail. "You can come over on Christmas Eve and help us trim it," he added generously.

"I'll like that," Gail said. "But for now, how about helping me trim this one?"

They used up the morning, ate sandwiches beneath the fragrant tree. Then Dave and Gail spent most of the afternoon on ladders, fastening strings of colored lights over and around the oaks on the front lawn.

"There must be a thousand yards of those lights," Alec said, eyeing the result. "You'll shine for miles."

"A Florida substitute for snow," Gail told him. "Glitter glamour. The trees will look like rainbow waterfalls tonight. We still have the ones in the back to do."

"I'll take them on," Alec offered. "Go help your mother with dinner."

"It's too early."

"Okay, grab a bat. We've got a baseball game planned."

Gail laughed and went in. Cooking wasn't her favorite thing, but it was way ahead of baseball.

"I SUPPOSE you've noticed that Bru is gaining weight," Virginia said smugly. "He was much too thin." Carrying dishes, she disappeared toward the dining room.

Standing at the back window, Gail watched her father swing a bat and send a baseball soaring. He took off in a lumbering run, stopped and laughed as Alec reached up and caught the ball deftly. Bru jumped up and down on the pitcher's mound and shrieked.

"Way to go, Dad! Never mind, Grandpa. Next time you'll slam it."

Gail turned away from the window laughing. It was just like Bru to cheer for both sides at once.

"Want me to call them in?" she asked as Virginia reappeared. "They'll want to wash up."

Peering into the oven, Virginia nodded. "You may as well." She straightened and turned her head toward the front of the house. "No, wait. That's the doorbell. I'll just turn this off until I see who it is—" She was gone again, her quick footsteps echoing in the hall.

Who came calling at dinnertime out here? Curious, Gail drifted toward the door to the hall.

"Yes," Virginia was saying politely. "This is the Winslow home. I'm Mrs. Winslow. How can I help you?"

"We're the Sommers," a man said authoritatively, "and we're looking for Dr. Alec Morgan. His answering service said he was here."

Gail gasped soundlessly and turned to look back through the kitchen window, instinctively wanting to

warn Alec, to grab Bru and run. She let out her breath,
trying to calm herself, and went into the hall, listening
to Virginia's flustered voice.

"Why, yes, he is. Come in, and I'll call him. He's outside in the back."

Gail watched them enter. Dick Sommers was well
fed, well dressed and barbered, but he had the loose lips
and the spider veins on his nose that marked a man who
drank too much. Louisa, plump and middle-aged, wore
an uncertain look and a thin wool suit that did its best
to hide a sagging figure. She fastened her gaze on Virginia and smiled with vague friendliness.

"We're terribly sorry to break in," she said. "But we
haven't much time, and we do need to see Alec." Her
gaze came up and alighted on Gail, traveled over her,
confused, and went back to Virginia. "Is Bruce with
him?"

Virginia caught on, and for an instant her face went
blank and fear shone in her green eyes. Recovering, she
smiled mechanically. "Yes, Bru's with him. Excuse me
a moment—I'll get them. This is my daughter, Gail
Sheridan. Gail, if you'll see that the Sommers are comfortable . . . ?"

"Of course," Gail said stiffly as Virginia fled. "Come
in by the fire, please. Would you like something to
drink? Coffee or a cup of tea?"

Dick Sommers coughed, moving toward the living
room. "Thank you, but no. If there's a spot of
brandy . . . ?"

"Yes, of course. Will you have one, Mrs. Sommers?"

"Oh, call me 'Louisa.' Yes, I suppose so, if everyone
else is." She scanned Gail again, from sneakers and
worn jeans to sweater and windblown hair. "Is Alec
here as, uh, your guest, Miss Sheridan?"

"*Mrs.* Sheridan," Gail said automatically. "Yes, he is," she added firmly. "And so is Bru. But this is my parents' house." She wondered suddenly why she was bothering with so much explanation.

She went to the liquor cabinet and took out a bottle of brandy. As she was reaching for glasses, she heard the back door slam. She turned, seeing them all come in, first Alec, then Bru and the Dobie, squeezing in together, stopping at the door. Bru's face was flushed from play, but as he stood there staring, he paled.

"Alec!" Louisa said, looking pleased. "How nice to see you. And Bruce! Come here, darling, and give Aunt Louisa a kiss."

Bruce swallowed hard. "I—I'd better not. I'm pretty dirty for kissing."

Sommers drew himself up. "Bruce," he said loudly, "don't be rude to your aunt! Your mother has sent us here to see that you're safe and in good health. Get over here and greet us both properly."

Bru's chin went up. "No. I'm living with my father now. You aren't supposed to boss me around."

"What?" Veins bulged in Dick's heavy neck; his eyes narrowed. "Well, I believe you need to show decent respect—" He took a step toward Bru, and suddenly the Dobie was in between them. Hackles rising, the dog lowered his head and fastened his eyes on Dick's chest, growled ominously and gathered his muscular body to leap. Everyone froze, and Gail gasped in horror.

"Puppy!" she snapped, "*Heel!*"

For a moment nothing happened. Then the growl died away, and the dog backed off slowly and took his place beside Gail's legs, his eyes still on Dick, his lip lifted in a silent snarl that exposed his long teeth.

"I wish," Bru said shakily into the silence, "that you wouldn't c-call Slash by that s-s-silly name, Gail."

Alec moved swiftly to Bru and put a hand on his shoulder. "She has to, son. Slash might have bitten someone. Stop worrying and go find Dave. I'll be back for you later." He gave Bru a pat and pushed him toward the door. Bru went, wiping at his eyes and breaking into a trot as he reached the hall. Alec turned to Dick, who still stood silent and shocked, staring at the dog.

"Come on, Dick," he said flatly. "We'll have our talk at my house."

Dick whirled to face him, the whites of his eyes showing. "I'm not moving an inch until someone chains that vicious dog!"

"I'll take him to the kitchen," Gail said quickly, and left, the Dobie close at her heels. Behind her, she heard Dick's voice, raised and angry.

"I'll sue, Morgan! You deliberately tried to intimidate me by bringing in that savage animal."

Gail shut the kitchen door and leaned against it, looking at Virginia, pale and sad, sitting at the table.

"I don't think we made a very good impression on Bru's aunt and uncle," she said carefully.

Virginia burst into tears. "Who cares? They'll take him away, Gail, and he doesn't even want to go. He went thorugh here on a run, looking for David."

Gail moved to the table and put an arm around her mother. "Don't cry, Mom. Maybe Alec can do something."

Virginia nodded and sat up. "I know he'll try. And we'll help if we can. At least he's still here for now. Hand me that box of tissues."

Gail handed over the box and wandered to the window to gaze out. Beside her, the Dobie whined, nosing at the door. Gail looked down at him.

"Lost somebody?" She patted him, then opened the door. "Go get 'em, Slash."

ALEC CAME BACK ALONE at twilight to pick up Gail and Bru. "The Sommers are waiting," he said in answer to the silent questions in everyone's eyes. "They want to have dinner with Bru and me. Then they'll leave. They'll be back after Christmas. Until then we go as we are. I'm sorry they upset your day."

He was very calm, Gail thought as they went out to the car. But other than that, there was no way of knowing what he was thinking. His expression reminded her of how he had appeared when they'd first met—closed off, reserved, remote. Alone. She had hoped—no, she had believed—that they had gotten past that stage, that he would be open about his fears and worries, talk them over with her. But, then, she thought, she should remember he didn't trust her. She looked down at Puppy, keeping pace with Bru.

"Would you rather I left the dog here?" she asked Alec.

"No," he answered abruptly, avoiding her eyes. "They won't be at your house. After tonight they won't even be in town until the day they pick up Bru. There's no reason to change your habits."

"They didn't like Slash, did they, Dad?" Bru's face was pinched and fearful. "Did you tell them he's not really mean?"

"Get in, son. We'll talk later."

Sliding into the car, Gail was quiet. Under Alec's calm she could sense a deep, frustrated anger moving, and she thought how galling it must be to have a man like Dick Sommers telling him what to do with his own son.

No one spoke until they drew up at Gail's house. "I'll be back," Alec said, staring through the windshield morosely, "but I don't know when. We're meeting at their motel and going out to dinner."

He wouldn't even look at her, let alone talk about the problem. She slid out and shut the door. "You don't need to bother, Alec. You have enough on your mind. I'm tired, anyway. I'll probably go to bed early."

Alec nodded, still not looking at her. "Good idea. I'll need some time on this, I suppose. See you later."

She glanced at him, the stiff face and shadowed eyes. Time. Maybe he did need time. But she wanted him to need her. Silently she turned toward the house. She would make no promises about later.

Inside, she headed for the shower. She wanted to help him, but he wouldn't even talk about his trouble. She was only for the happy times, the easy times.

Stepping out of the shower, reaching for a towel, she thought of the day they had argued about the premarital agreement and Alec had tried to explain. "It damn near killed me to lose Bru," he had said. "I couldn't stand it happening twice."

In a way it *was* happening twice. It would be even worse having to let Bru go back when he knew he'd be unhappy. The pain in her chest grew; anger at Bru's thoughtless mother tensed her muscles. She decided that this must be why some people kidnapped their own children and disappeared. And to be fair, maybe it was why some people made out premarital agreements—so it couldn't happen again.

A TAPPING at Gail's bedroom window woke her from a sound sleep. She sat up and saw through the shadowy curtains a large, familiar form silhouetted by pale moonlight. Turning on a light, she slipped out, threw on a robe and went to unlock the front door.

Coming in, Alec brought a draft of cold air. Gail shut the door hurriedly, wrapped her robe tighter and turned to face him, tossing back her tangled hair. She was still a little angry at being shut out. "Isn't it a trifle late for visiting?"

"I'm sorry," Alec said gently, taking off his coat. "You must be tired after a day like this. I know I am."

Her eyes searched his face, the dark hollows beneath his hooded eyes, the new lines in his flat cheeks. Her expression softened and her stiff mouth relaxed into tenderness.

"You should have gone straight to bed, Alec."

He dropped his coat on the nearest chair and took her in his arms, kissing her sleep-warmed cheeks, her drowsy eyes. "I couldn't. I needed to be with you." He parted her robe and slipped his chilled hands inside, feeling the warmth of her body through the thin silk of her gown. He let out his breath and pulled her close, kissing her again. "Gail...I was...just going to talk..."

Gail was acutely aware of cold and hot. His icy hands on her warm back; the chilled, bristly cheek against hers. The quickening, urgent heat of his body; the fire that leaped and danced and ran through her veins. She drew in a deep breath and gave up any thought of reasoning or argument.

"Come to bed," she said huskily. "We'll talk later."

They were gentle with each other, and tender. It was as if they were two survivors of a terrible disaster, overwhelmed with joy at finding each other again, safe and unharmed.

"Even my skin was hungry for you," Alec said, holding her full length against him, stroking her back. "I had made up my mind to keep you out of this problem, to leave you alone until I solved it, but sitting there with those pompous fools I ached all over. I could think of nothing but how you would feel to me when I held you like this again."

"I know," Gail murmured. "My arms felt empty. I was lonely." It was true, but it was much more than that. She had thought she would have to give him up, and now she had begun to hope again. Maybe he would begin to trust her; maybe he would let her in. "Darling," she whispered, kissing him. "I'm so glad you came back to me."

By now they each knew the touches, the words, the subtle caresses that were magic to the other one, and they used them all to fuel the fire between them. In the end the words became wild and incoherent, the fire out of control, consuming them breathlessly at the ultimate peak.

They lay there, silent and content, until the cool night air reminded them to pull up the covers and huddle together.

"I thought I was losing you," Alec whispered, and Gail smiled, weaving her fingers through the crisp curls on his chest.

"I thought you were already gone."

"Why?"

"I suppose because you went away inside your mind. It was like some stranger had moved into your body."

Alec groaned. "I was trying to protect you, but I couldn't stay away. I had to get back to you. Talk to you. What I've learned about this situation frightens me."

"*Frightens* you?"

"Yes. It's far worse than I thought. Dick Sommers is acting from a position of real strength—Marian has *hired* them to take over Bru's care and discipline, and you've seen how he is. He's a drunk." Alec twisted restlessly and sat up, looking down at her in the dim light. "Louisa let it drop that they've found another, even more exclusive school, with all kinds of precautions to prevent runaways. She says it's a wonderful place where Bru will be 'perfectly safe,' and in the summer she and Dick are going to take him to Europe."

"Oh, *no!*"

"Oh, yes," Alec said grimly. "And I'm not sure they can't do it. I've got to get a lawyer."

"Now wait a minute! Surely Bru's mother will listen to *Bru.* If he tells her he's miserable with the Sommers—"

"She knows that," Alec broke in. "Louisa told me there had been trouble before between Dick and Bru, but that Marian felt Bru could stand a little discipline."

Gail stared. "Then why doesn't *she* apply it?"

"According to Louisa, Marian is too busy entertaining Hewlett's important business contacts to watch over an active nine-year-old boy."

"Oh, Alec, don't *listen* to her! She must be lying. No mother would feel like that." Gail sat up with him, holding him, trying to comfort him, wondering painfully if what she had just said was right. "Surely," she added as a shocked afterthought, "Louisa didn't say all those things in front of Bru?"

"Yes, she did," Alec said slowly. "She acted as if he should be grateful for all the great things they were doing for him. And Bru didn't fuss. He just sat, minding his manners, and never said a word."

"That's not like Bru."

"No." Alec turned his head, staring at the tiny lamp on the dresser, rubbing his chin with its day's growth of golden beard. "I have been so damn stupid, Gail. I asked Louisa if Marian ever spent any time with Bru, and she stared at me as if I should know better and said, 'Why, of course. She sees him at breakfast when both of them are at home. But Marian has never been interested in children's activities. That's why she hired us.'"

Gail drew in her breath. "Did Bru hear that?"

Alec turned back to her with a wintry smile. "Sure. He paid no attention to it at all. As I said, I'm the one who's been stupid. Bru *knows*. I suppose he's always known. Children are hard to fool."

Tears misted Gail's eyes. "Poor Bru," she said softly. "No wonder he ran away to you."

"I'm not much better," Alec said abruptly. "I let my own problems blind me to Bru's. I knew he depended on me for attention and fun, and I should have insisted on full custody from the beginning. Now I'm in for a battle I could lose." His face was tense again, his thick brows furrowed. "With Hewlett's lawyers behind her, Marian will be hard to beat."

Gail slid from the bed and grabbed her robe, her face suddenly shining. "You're going to fight for him, aren't you? Wonderful! I'll help you, in every way I can. Let's go make coffee and think...."

Staring at her, Alec smiled, the furrows in his forehead smoothing out. He grabbed her around the waist and swept her back into bed again. "We'll think when we know what to think about," he said, pressing her down as she laughed and tried to rise again. "I need to do some investigating first. In the meantime, let's stay with something we know will be a success."

11

VIRGINIA WINSLOW'S CALL woke Gail from an exhausted sleep shortly after eight the next morning.

"Your father and I want to know what's going to happen," Virginia said. "We couldn't sleep for worrying about it."

Sleepy and confused, Gail sorted through what she had learned from Alec last night, looking for something she could safely say. There was nothing. "I don't know what Alec is going to do," she answered foggily.

"Well," Virginia snapped nervously, "you won't find out lying around in bed. I can tell you just woke up, and it's almost eight-thirty. Don't you care what happens to Bru?"

Gail stared at the ceiling for a full minute, willing herself to patience. It didn't work.

"That is just about enough out of you. Both Alec and I are grown up people, not idiot children. And you're being obnoxious." She winced and lowered the phone to the cradle. Virginia had hung up with a crash. Maybe she didn't appreciate hearing the truth. But at least her mother hadn't dissolved into tears. There was still a lot of fight there. She swung from the bed and went to let Puppy out and start a pot of coffee.

She was dressed and on her first cup when someone knocked. Opening the door, she found Bru with his fist raised to knock again. He grinned at her and lowered his hand.

"Dad said that if it's all right with you I can play with Slash for fifteen minutes. Is it all right with you?"

Gail laughed, her spirits rising. "If it's all right with Slash. He's in the backyard. Go ask him."

Bru grinned and was gone, flying through the room and down the hall. Gail went back to her coffee, glancing at the clock and reflecting that if the fifteen minutes ran overtime, she'd be late for her first appointment. Which also was all right with her. Bru needed that dog. Now that he'd started school, he'd soon make some human friends—that is, if he got to stay. But for now that Dobie filled the gap. She smiled, listening to laughter and shouts, the thump of a ball. Somehow, during what must have been a lonely time, Bru had learned to make the most of what happiness he could find.

Exactly fourteen and a half minutes later, Bru and the dog came in through the door together.

"Right on time," Gail said, surprised.

"Sure. Dad lent me his watch." Bru displayed it, high on his arm. "Thanks, Gail. Maybe I'll see you later." He hesitated, his green eyes troubled. "Did you know my aunt and uncle might take me back to Chicago?"

Suddenly speechless, Gail nodded.

Bru looked at his shoes. "If they do, will you tell Grandpa and Grandma goodbye for me? And tell them I'll see them next summer?"

Gail swallowed. "I'm sure you'll have time to tell them yourself, Bru. But if you don't, I certainly will. They'll be very glad to see you when you come back."

Bru's grin was uncannily like Alec's. "So will I. Be glad to see them, I mean. See you, Gail. Bye, Slash." He was gone again; an instant later the front door closed and Puppy whined mournfully.

"Damn those people," Gail said aloud, and got up to go call her mother. After all, she could tell her that so far nothing stood in the way of a Merry Christmas. But perhaps she'd better follow that by warning her not to count on a Happy New Year.

AT NOON Alec and Bru were waiting at Gail's door when she drove up. Bru's face was bright in the winter sunshine, and he was grinning like a reprieved prisoner.

"We came after the dog," Alec said as she got out and came toward them. "Bru's teacher said he could start the Christmas vacation early, and he wants to spend it with Ginny and Dave."

"Wonderful." Gail looked away, fumbling for a key. Alec was smiling, but under the smile his face looked drawn and tired. Gail's hand shook as she unlocked the door. "Go get him, Bru." She turned to Alec as Bru ran in. "What happened?"

"Nothing. I just decided he'd be better off out there, staying busy and outdoors." He hesitated, coloring slightly as she met his eyes. "Okay. That isn't all of it. I guess I'm running scared. It's only an hour and a half by air from here to the Bahamas, and I wouldn't put it past Dick Sommers to pull a sneak and pick him up at school."

Gail started to speak, but she heard Bru coming up behind her.

He appeared with a leashed Puppy. "I locked the back door because I'm taking your guard. Okay?"

"Okay," Gail said, "Let's go. I'm riding out with you. I want to see Virginia's face."

Virginia's face wore an ecstatic expression. She insisted that they come in and see what David had made for Bru. "You'll love it," she said, taking Bru's hand. "But you'll have to take care of it. It's one of a kind."

In the kitchen, David handed over a beautifully carved and polished walnut replica of a Doberman standing at attention, ears pricked. Awed, Bru took it reverently in both hands and stroked the satiny back. "It's exactly like Slash, Grandpa. I'll keep it forever."

David grinned. "Promise to feed him a little furniture polish once in a while?"

"You bet! I'll keep him shiny. He's beautiful."

Drawing Alec aside, Virginia said, "Under the circumstances, can Bru stay out here until after Christmas? That would give us a wonderful holiday."

"I was just about to ask *you*," Alec said gently. "That would be great if he's not too much trouble."

"Humph," Virginia snorted. "We'd steal him if we could. You two go on about your business. He's safe with us."

Alec headed south when they left. "It's as good a time as any to show you the house," he said, slanting a glance at Gail. "If only to point out that life with me wouldn't be all trouble."

Gail let the remark pass. "Speaking of trouble," she said. "Tell me why you believe Dick Sommers might kidnap Bru?"

Alec gave her a sardonic look. "It wouldn't be kidnapping, or he'd never dare. Under the circumstances, he would have every right to take Bru wherever he found him, and he just might prefer to search him out at school and avoid me. But if I have to let Bru go, I want to be sure he understands and knows I'll be trying to get him back."

"I see," Gail said. "And I wish I didn't. This time the law is on the wrong side."

"I'm working on that. I called my lawyer in New York and he's looking into it." Slowing the car, Alec brightened. "Look, there's the house. Still just a shell, but you can see what it's going to be like."

Sprawled on the rolling slope between the woods and the lake, the multilevel home with its rambling walls of stone and wood was big enough for a large family. Trucks were parked on the graded road leading in; men swarmed around the site, carrying in rolls of insulation and paneling. The sound of hammering was constant. Even with the half-finished roof and raw, unstained wood, the house was handsome, the design perfect for the site.

Gail looked at it soberly. Until now, the house had had no reality; it had been only Alec's fantasy of a place for her and Bru and the other children he wanted. But here it was, solid proof that he meant what he said. And what she felt most was guilt. But why? He'd have no trouble finding another woman to make this house a home.

"It's beautiful, Alec. I'm impressed."

His arms crossed on the steering wheel, his chin resting on his wrists, Alec peered through the windshield at the house and smiled. "Wait until it's finished. You won't be able to resist moving in." But this time there was a touch of bravado in his voice, as if he had a few doubts he didn't want to recognize. "Bru can't wait. He's already picked out a place for a tree house back in the woods." He leaned back and started the car again. "We'll come back on Sunday, when the men aren't working, and let him show you the room he wants."

"Fine," Gail said, and hurriedly looked at her watch. "Lunch will have to be fast food," she added, changing the subject. "Both of us are late."

"Right." He swung the car in a wide U-turn and started back along the deserted road, reaching across to cup her silken knee in his broad palm. "We're free, angel. For twenty-four hours there's no one but you and me. Let's make the most of it."

Gail smiled, thinking of Bru and his fifteen minutes. Maybe it was a Morgan trait to make the most of what they had. "Sounds wonderful," she said lightly. "Come over at six and I'll cook dinner."

"You come over and I'll cook," Alec said expansively. "I miss seeing you surrounded by Persian blue."

The last words triggered the memory of their first night together. "My woman," he'd said. "Now and forever." So there would be no forever, but there was the now. She couldn't, or wouldn't, desert him until he and Bru settled. The Morgan trait suddenly seemed eminently wise. Make the most of it.

"Promise me no invaders," she said, "and I'll be there."

Alec laughed. "I promise. We'll be alone."

DETERMINED THAT THE EVENING should be special, Gail pushed aside the casual clothes in her closet and took out a new silk dress of iridescent blue-green that flowed around her when she walked, marking the curves and hollows of her body with varying, subtle shades of color. It fitted the mood, she decided, by making the most of what she had.

The dress demanded makeup to accent her eyes, a spray of her most tantalizing scent, and the small emerald earrings she hadn't worn for years. Checking the mirror, she smiled, put on her coat and went out into winter twilight, locking her door and turning to find

Alec coming toward her from the street. She laughed and took his arm.

"Nice," she said. "But you didn't have to come for me. I thought you'd be juggling pots and pans."

He stopped in the shadow of a tree and kissed her lightly. "A woman wearing emeralds and that perfume isn't safe even in broad daylight. And dinner is ready, when we want to eat. The evening lies before us, *madame*. Let's hurry."

She laughed, trying to match his long stride. "If dinner is ready, you're either madly efficient or we're having hot dogs."

"Efficient. I called the Castillo Restaurant at four and they delivered the dinner fifteen minutes ago. A quick pass through the microwave is all it needs."

They were still laughing as they neared his house. But the laughter died when they saw a limousine parked in front of his door. Two men stood under the rose trellis over the entry.

"Now who in the hell..." Alec said under his breath, and slowed. "Let's cut around to the back."

"Too late," Gail whispered. "They've seen us. One is coming this way."

A large man wearing a topcoat and a hat pushed through the gate. "Dr. Alec Morgan?"

"That's right," Alec said, irritated. "But I don't have evening office hours. Is this an emergency?"

The man smiled, tipping his hat to Gail. "No, sir, it isn't. You have a caller—Roger Hewlett. Mr. Hewlett is waiting at your door."

After a moment of intense silence, Alec spoke reluctantly. "In that case, I suppose I'd better let him in."

"Yes, sir. I'll wait in the car."

"Suit yourself," Alec said, still irritated. "But it's warm inside."

"Thank you, but the car is heated."

"I promised you," Alec muttered, going up the path. "No invaders. I'd like to throw him out."

Gail squeezed his arm. "Be careful, Alec. He could be either friend or foe. Give him a chance."

Hewlett, shapeless in hat, muffler and topcoat, was small. He moved slightly to one side as they came up the steps, then offered a gloved hand.

"Dr. Morgan." His voice was husky with age but pleasant. His face was thin and lined, with a strong hooked nose and thin mouth. His eyes, colorless in the dim light, were large and thoughtful. There was something Old World about him, something European, from the long ago.

"Mr. Hewlett." Alec shook his hand briefly and turned to Gail. "Gail Sheridan, Mr. Hewlett."

Hewlett inclined his head. "I see you had more pleasant plans for the evening than talking to me. I won't keep you long."

"Fine," Alec said pointedly. "Just let me unlock the door."

Inside, Hewlett removed his hat and topcoat, revealing thick white hair and a slender but straight body in a dark suit. He looked with surprise at the reception room and desk, laid his coat and hat on a chair and fixed his gaze on Alec. "This is your home, Doctor, as well as your offices?"

Alec grinned suddenly. "Not what you expected, Hewlett?"

"Of course it isn't," Hewlett said. "I investigated you thoroughly, and I know what you're worth. But, then, how you choose to live isn't my business, now is it? Tell me, where are Dick and Louisa Sommers?"

"Your guess is probably better than mine," Alec said warily. "Did you think they were here?"

"I know they were. The information became available to me twenty-four hours ago. I want to know where they are now."

Alec let out his breath and shrugged. "Vacationing in the islands. I don't know which island, but I suppose you do."

"Is Bruce with them?"

Gail moved nervously, taking off her coat, watching the blood climb Alec's neck. "Why don't you sit down?" she said, to give Alec time to calm himself. "Right here, Mr. Hewlett. This chair is comfortable."

The large eyes moved to her, ran over her appraisingly and warmed. The thin mouth curled in a singularly sweet smile. "Thank you, I am tired. Keeping up with my wife's plans becomes more wearing and less interesting every day." He sat down and turned again to Alec. "Well, *is* Bruce with them?"

"No."

Hewlett smiled. "That eases my mind. I can't imagine what Marian was thinking of, sending Dick Sommers for the boy. Is Bruce here?"

"No."

"A pity. I'd hoped to see him. I'm curious about how he got away from that school and made his way down here, but I suppose you won't tell me."

"That's right," Alec said. "But I will tell you that he had no help from me. I didn't know he was coming."

"Such an enterprising lad," Hewlett said admiringly. "I can't say I blame him. It is a very dull school, though safe. However, that is neither here nor there. I should be asking your pardon for the trouble he has caused you."

Alec turned red. "Trouble? He's my son, Hewlett. I'm delighted to have him with me."

"I'm glad to hear it. One never knows these days. Modern families tend to give their children everything but their time. Now in my day—but why talk of the past? My sons are good men, good businessmen. I'm going to leave them everything I have. Marian will get only a trust fund, smaller than the one you gave her."

Surprised, Alec gave up his aggressive stand and sat down, staring at the old man. "That is certainly none of my business, but I suppose you have some reason for telling me."

"Of course," Hewlett said calmly. "I think it fair to let you know your son will not inherit any part of the Hewlett fortune. And if you're thinking Marian will be able to break my will, think again. I'm old, but I'm not a fool. I saw to it that she signed a premarital agreement."

"I see." Alec's eyes shot to Gail's, but her head was bent, her gaze on her clasped hands. She did not look up. "I'm surprised," he said to Hewlett. "I would have thought Marian would object."

The old man sighed. "She did. Violently. But I insisted. With a woman like Marian, it's a necessary move. And all in all, I've been satisfied with my bargain. She's an excellent hostess and a pleasant companion when I'm at home."

"Let's get back to Bruce," Alec said grimly.

"Why? I plan no changes there. Marian is his mother and it's up to her if she wants to keep him."

Alec turned red again. "You've indicated that you like Bru, but you're not being fair to him. He'd be better off with me. Marian isn't even a good imitation of a mother."

Hewlett smiled again. "You're exaggerating, Morgan, but not much. She does seem to have very little maternal feeling except for pride in having produced him. Still, she's my wife and she wants him. I never let the Hewlett side down." He rose, picked up his hat and coat and put them on. "Don't worry, I keep an eye on Bruce myself. For instance, I know Dick Sommers too well to let him handle the boy, so I'll be with them when they come for him. And, of course, I'll see that Bruce is sent to you for the summer. Dick was just using him in the hope of gaining a trip to Europe for himself."

Alec got to his feet, still trying to hide his anger. "I appreciate that, Hewlett, but I still want full custody. If I have to, I'll take the matter to court."

"My favorite arena," Hewlett said placidly. "And I'm sure you know you can't win." He turned and smiled at Gail. "It's been a pleasure, Miss Sheridan."

"Thank you," Gail said, wondering wryly what pleasure he might find in his subtle threats. "I'm sorry I can't say the same. I had hoped we could keep Bru here."

Hewlett's cynical humor faded. "I'm sorry, too, my dear. It's an unfortunate situation. Good night, Dr. Morgan. Remember, I'll want the boy ready soon after Christmas."

Outside, the car door slammed as Hewlett opened the front door, and the chauffeur came hurrying up to take Hewlett's arm.

"Careful of the steps, sir. They're a bit uneven."

Alec shut the door and turned back to Gail, bewildered and furious. "I wish he'd trip and break his neck.

He knows I'm right, but he's still going to fight me. The man is sadistic!"

"Eccentric, I think," Gail said faintly. "Even weird. But I think he does like Bru. And he wants to give Marian what she wants. Aside from that, I guess Hewletts have to come out on top."

"At this point, I don't think he's got much to worry about," Alec said grimly.

Gail was afriad to ask what that meant. "Let's go up," she said, instead. "I could do with a drink after this."

Upstairs, Alec poured drinks, gave one to Gail and settled down with her on the long couch.

"What a miserable start for our evening. I'm sorry, angel. You must be tired of my problems."

"Don't be silly. I'm as worried about Bru as you are."

"I should thank Hewlett for taking a stand against Sommers. If Bru has to go back for a while he can handle it now. He's a game kid, and he'll have the summer to look forward to."

"Don't even say that," Gail protested, shuddering. "Bru doesn't need any more of that life."

"I know." Alec ran a hand through his hair, his face pale in the aftermath of anger. "But unless we can think of something between now and their return he'll have to go with them. Legal action takes time, and until we win they're in control."

Gail had no answer for that. She nodded mutely, sipped at her drink and then set it down. "Where are those dinners? No one can think on an empty stomach, and we have to think."

"Finish your drink," Alec said. "I'll take care of dinner. Maybe we don't know enough to do any thinking.

I'll call New York again and see what my lawyer has found out."

Picking up her glass, Gail followed Alec to the dining area and sat at the already laid table, watching as he moved around in the open kitchen, his hair bronze in the overhead light, his broad shoulders and tall, muscular body looking out of place in the domestic scene.

"I can do that," she said gently. "Come sit down."

He glanced at her and smiled. "Think I can't? I'm a master at warming things up in the microwave. Sit there and be a guest."

She sat, studying him, and finally she had to ask, "You aren't going to give up, are you?"

"No, of course not," Alec replied, deftly removing a platter from the small oven. "If I lose, I lose, but I won't give up. Things may change."

Gail looked at him forlornly, thinking of Bru, thinking of her parents, of Puppy. All lonely at once. "I don't see how. It looks hopeless to me."

"Wait." He brought over the platter laden with steaming shrimp scampi and put it between them, then went back to bring salads and wine from the refrigerator. Sitting down, he studied her puzzled face and smiled.

"Think, angel. Marian hired the Sommers so she could get out of any responsibility for Bru. Old Hewlett thinks she should take care of Bru herself. If they disagree about that there may be other problems. I'll set up an investigation."

Gail looked at him thoughtfully, then nodded. "It could make a difference, I suppose. But how do we take advantage of it?"

Alec's face lighted up. "Bless you. I like that 'we.' I have no idea how, but together we're bound to think of something. Now let's make the most of what time we have left tonight."

12

IT WAS AFTER MIDNIGHT when Gail slid quietly from Alec's bed and began to dress. Eyes still closed, Alec groaned.

"We'd get more sleep if we were married."

Gail smiled. "And even more if we'd never met." She wasn't getting into that discussion again.

Alec sat up. "I refuse to consider that possibility." Climbing out of bed, he began putting on his clothes to walk her home. His sleepy eyes warmed as they ran over her. "Darling, what a beautiful dress. It looks wonderful on you."

"Next time you invite me to a special dinner, I'll wear my jeans," Gail said indignantly. "My old jeans. I slithered around all evening in this and you never noticed it."

"I didn't notice the dress, but I noticed you."

She laughed, relenting. "I guess that's better. Anyway, the dress made an impression on Roger Hewlett. He gave it a lecherous look. What a funny old man he is."

"About as funny as a rattlesnake. I'd hate to make him mad."

As she put on her coat and went to the stairs, Gail was silent. But walking home in the cold air, she shivered and spoke. "'United we stand,'" she quoted softly, "'divided...they fall.' Let's have a rally, Alec. It's time to let my parents in on this."

He looked at her curiously. "What can they do?"

"Who knows? For one thing, we can count on them to keep Bru with them until we work out a plan. And there might be other things. You know they'll do anything to help you keep him."

Alec nodded, going into her house with her to check the rooms. With the Dobie at the Winslows, he worried a little. Then, still in his topcoat, he held her close before he left. "If you want them to know, tell them. It can't hurt. But what gave you that idea?"

"It's a battle," Gail said. "So we need a united front and a divided enemy. I'm uniting the front. Maybe the Sommers will divide the enemy."

Alec laughed. "You sound like a budding subversive. I hope it'll work. But it seems that Hewlett's tolerance knows no bounds when it comes to Marian and what Marian wants."

Gail sighed and kissed him. "You're probably right. It was just a thought. Good night, my love."

Walking home, Alec was still thinking about Gail's idea. A good one, if it weren't for Hewlett's amazing acceptance of Marian's faults. Still, the old man was proud. He was proud of his name, his fortune and his power. Marian probably had to toe the line when it came to what Hewlett said. Turning in at his gate, Alec suddenly wondered how long Hewlett's ignorance would last if his pride were hurt.

BEFORE LEAVING for work the next morning, Gail called her parents' home. "Mom?"

"It's you. You're making me burn Bru's pancakes. Don't you have to work?"

"Just leaving for my first appointment. I called to say we'll be out this evening to bring Bru some clothes and tell you our plans."

Virginia snorted. "What an occasion. Miss Mumlips is finally going to speak."

"You're impossible," Gail said with a flash of temper, and hung up on her. Getting into her car, she consulted her list of waiting clients. Too long. If she wanted to have a business when this was over, she'd have to put more time in.

Three first interviews today, she remembered. Those crucial discussions when she discovered the client's preferences in styles, colors and fabrics. And one second interview, when she offered rough sketches and samples, neither of which she had yet. She groaned and headed for Coleman's. Lena had enlarged her shop to include samples of wallpaper and drapery material.

Home again for lunch, Gail made a sandwich and a cup of coffee, spread her work on the coffee table and worked on sketches while she ate. She switched on her recorder, playing back a tape to refresh her memory of what the client had said she liked in drapery styles.

The chatty voice was still talking when the sound of a knock made Gail stop the Play function and hurry to open the door. Standing there, Alec looked hesitant.

"You aren't alone, are you? I'll come back later."

"There's no one here," Gail said, surprised, and then laughed. "I know—you heard my recorder. That's only one of my clients expressing her views on Roman draperies. Thank heaven she doesn't like them. Come in. Did you talk to your lawyer?"

Shrugging out of his coat, Alec kissed her, then drew her with him to the small couch, ignoring the litter of papers and sketches, and the now silent recorder.

"Yes, for close to an hour. He wasn't much help." Leaning back, Alec looked tired and depressed. "He knows Roger Hewlett. Also, he knows two of Hewlett's lawyers. He says we'll need solid evidence of abuse and neglect to have a case, and he wouldn't guarantee success even then."

"Bru *was* neglected," Gail flared. "Stuck in that school most of the year just to keep him out of the house! And if a lack of love and attention isn't abuse, I don't know what is."

"I know. But it might be hard to convince a judge that enrolling a child in an expensive private school is neglect. And how do you prove the rest of it? Put Marian on the stand, and she'll swear she adores her child. Who doubts a mother?"

After a long moment, Gail nodded soberly. "You'd lose."

"And that isn't all. From what I hear, Hewlett never fails to countersue. If he could prove to the judge's satisfaction that I harbored Bru as a runaway and kept Dick from taking him, I might lose what small amount of time with Bru I have. No summers."

"Oh, Alec, you can't risk that."

"Exactly. Without more evidence I'll have to forget it."

As he spoke, Gail noticed the tiny red light flicker on the recorder. "Good Lord, I forgot to turn off this thing. I'll erase it. Our conversation doesn't belong in my work records."

"It wasn't on, angel."

Gail turned the recorder so the light was toward him. "Watch."

The tiny light blinked on and off as she said the word. Alec's brows went up. "Voice activated? I've heard about those, but I've never seen one." The light blinked again as he spoke, and Gail smiled, reached forward and played the tape back for him, then erased it and turned the machine off.

"See? It's great for my work. I ask questions and my clients answer, and there's no interference and no blank spaces. The tape doesn't run if no one is speaking. Of course I do it legally—tell them first that I'm recording—but they don't mind. A regular recorder puts them off because they can hear it. I think the noise makes them self-conscious and they don't always say what they mean—" She stopped, looking at him ruefully. "I'm boring you."

Alec smiled and kissed her. "You couldn't. But I guess I can't think of anything else but my own problems right now. Which reminds me, I have patients waiting. Pick you up at four?"

"I'll be ready." She went to the door and watched his long-legged stride quickly take him the short distance to his house in a matter of a minute, then turned and went back to her own work with a building determination to do something—anything—to help keep Bru here where he belonged.

AT TEN MINUTES to four, at home and relaxed in jeans and coddling tired feet in padded jogging shoes, Gail felt hopeful but still confused. Plans and plots ran circles in her mind like hamsters on a treadmill. None made any sense. When Alec drove up she ran out and hopped into the old BMW, leaned back and shook her head.

"I'm of no use at all. I can't think of anything short of murder that will work."

Alec reached for her hand and held it as he drove. "Nor I. We're probably trying too hard. The situation is loaded, angel, and mostly from my stupidity. I let Marian get the divorce on trumped-up evidence, when I could have divorced her for infidelity. I let her keep Bru because she had a home and I didn't yet. I was . . . chivalrous, I guess you'd say, making it look good for the lady. Whatever, I did it. Now, when Bru's miserable there, I can't help him!"

The last words came out between gritted teeth, punctuated by Alec's fist banging on the steering wheel. "And, dammit," he added savagely, "I'm beginning to see she doesn't even like being around children."

Gail stared at him. "That's foolish, Alec. She's his *mother*. And Bru is a superlative son. Good-looking and intelligent. She must be proud of him."

Alec sighed. "She is. She always showed him off— and then sent him away with the maid. I thought when I wasn't around to spend time with him, she would. But evidently she doesn't."

"Then why," Gail asked slowly, "is she so determined to keep him? You'd think she'd hand him over like a shot and just see him on holidays, the way you're supposed to."

Alec shrugged. "All I know is that my lawyer says she complains that Bru is becoming 'unmanageable,' but still absolutely refuses to give me custody."

Gail sighed. "You can't argue without any arguing point, and evidently she's not going to give us one. We're almost there. How much do you want to tell my parents?"

"I'll get Bru out of the way and leave what to say up to you."

"To Miss Mumlips," Gail said, and laughed.

"What?"

"Oh, nothing. Look, there's Bru, waving and running to meet us."

"And Ginny coming down the steps," Alec said. "This is one place I always feel welcome." He sounded immensely grateful.

Inside, Gail handed Virginia a bundle of clothes and Virginia trotted off to put them in the bedroom now classified as Bru's.

"I'll take Bru outside and find Dave," Alec said. "I'll send him in to see you, and Bru and I will take a walk in the woods, huh, Bru?"

"Sure! I'll show you a bird's nest I found. It's okay to look in it, it's empty." Bru took Alec's hand and tugged. "Grandpa says it's a redbird nest. Or was."

Virginia bustled back in as they left, waited until they shut the back door, then turned to Gail. "Shall we hide him if his aunt and uncle show up?"

Gail laughed. "Now I know why I have criminal impulses. I inherited them. No, we can't go that far. Wait until Dad comes in. . . ."

"I'm here," Dave said from the door. "I saw you drive up. What is all this, Gail?"

"Trouble," Gail said. "Alec and I decided you ought to know." She frowned. "Some of it's unbelievable and some is too personal, so it goes no farther than the two of you. Sit down."

She told them first about the illuminating visit of Roger Hewlett, about his evident concern for Bru and his calm determination to keep Bru for Marian.

"There is no real evidence of abuse, then," Dave said heavily. "And Roger Hewlett is a very wealthy and influential man. What are you going to do, Gail?"

Gail hesitated. "We honestly don't know," she said. "They won't be here until after Christmas, so we've time to think. Alec's lawyer doesn't give us much chance in the courts, so we'll be thinking hard."

Dave ran a hand through his shock of silver hair. "It's a damn pity. Bru asks me every day if he can stay a little longer. I think he's really worried about going back."

"Why wouldn't he be?" Gail said softly. "He's happier here than he's ever been in his life. It'll be harder than ever to go back now. But Alec is fighting to keep him—maybe he'll win."

"What can *we* do?" Virginia burst out. "Whatever it is, we'll do it. Even if we have to lie! Won't we, Dave?"

"Anything," Dave said calmly. "Short of murder."

Gail laughed. "Exactly what Alec said, Dad. But all we need from you two is what you're doing now."

"When will he have to leave," Virginia asked fearfully, "On New Year's?"

"I don't know, Mom. Maybe. All they say is that they'll come for him after Christmas." She looked toward the hall, hearing the scrabble of Puppy's feet in the kitchen. "They're here," she cautioned. The Dobie bounded in and came to sit, trembling with excitement, beside her chair.

"Slash wanted to see you, Gail," Bru said, coming in behind him. He went over to her chair and looked at her soberly. "He's really your dog, isn't he?"

"He's *our* dog," Gail said, and put an arm around Bru's thin shoulders. "And he knows it. It's only that when he's with you, he misses me, and when he's with me, he misses you."

Bru leaned on the arm of her chair. "Does he, Gail? Does he really miss me?"

"You know he does. He howls when you leave."

Bru put his head on her shoulder. His bronze curls smelled like fresh air and pine, like soap and boy. "He howls when you leave, too. That proves we ought to live in the same house."

Gail's breath caught in her throat. The same house. It sounded so right. After a moment she put her other arm around him and hugged. Looking up, she saw that Alec had come in and was grinning down at her. He leaned over and rumpled Bru's hair.

"That's what I keep telling her, Bru. But I never thought of Slash as a reason. Keep that in mind, Gail. You want the dog happy, don't you?"

Thank heaven he was keeping things light. Gail smiled at him gratefully. "It's a point," she conceded. "But he's happy here with Bru to play with. Aren't you, Puppy?"

"Slash," Bru corrected, and straigthened. "Puppy's a baby name. Want to see him catch a ball?"

"We all do," Dave said, getting up. "It'll do us good. Come on, Ginny."

GOING HOME LATE, Alec asked Gail if Bru had interrupted her conversation with her parents. "I looked around and he was gone, running like the wind after the dog, who'd been whining to go back ever since we started into the woods. Bru was right, I think. Puppy knew you'd come and wanted to see you."

"Slash," Gail said, and grinned. "No, he didn't interrupt. We were really through talking. Just hashing over what could happen. Then I heard them in the kitchen and we all shut up."

Alec looked at her curiously. "Do you think he heard anything that was said?"

"No." She frowned. "At least, I hope not. Dad says Bru's worried about having to leave. But Bru didn't say anything except about the dog."

"Then he didn't overhear anything," Alec said comfortably. "Bru comes out with what he's thinking. How did Dave and Ginny react to what you told them?"

Gail laughed. "Mom's ready to perjure herself in your favor. Dad will do anything short of murder. We aren't alone."

"I was sure they'd feel that way. They're wonderful people." He reached for her hand, groping in the dark to find it, then clasped it tightly. "With a wonderful daughter. Are you going to make your dog happy?"

It took her a moment, then she sighed. "Considering the trouble you're having from your last wife, I can't imagine why you want another one. Aren't you ever going to give up?"

"Nope."

The word had a sort of cheerful finality, and Gail left the matter at that. This was not a time to argue about the future. The present held problems enough. At the same time, an errant question filtered through her concern for Alec and Bru and startled her. How would she feel if he'd said yes?

"We're going to your house," Alec said later, turning onto Charlotte Street. "Mine is like a desert without Bru. In fact, I may stay with you all night."

Leaning on his shoulder, Gail yawned contentedly. "You'll have to get up awfully early to beat Mrs. Langford. She picks up her morning paper by flashlight."

"Then I'll stay and pretend I dropped in early for breakfast."

They had never spent a whole night together. Her fault, of course. She'd wanted to maintain her feeling of separate lives. But now she thought of waking in the morning with Alec beside her, warm and tousled and intimate, and her resistance melted. Who knew how much time they might have together? They would make the most of tonight. She sat up and smiled.

"Park behind your place then, and we'll walk to mine. If my landlady sees your car in front of my door at five a.m., she'll never believe you just dropped in."

Alec laughed. "Would she put you out?"

"Like a shot. She has a rule—no single tenant has overnight guests of the opposite sex."

"She's living in the past," Alec said, pulling into his backyard. "But I can solve that little problem. If she puts you out, I'll take you in."

"Fine," Gail answered lightly, getting out. "Then we'll ruin your reputation with all those senior citizens you treat. They'll think it's awful that you're living in sin."

He came around the car, laughing, and took her arm. "In that case, I'll have to make an honest woman of you."

She glanced up at him and frowned faintly. He never missed a chance to promote marriage. She let it pass and started around the house with him. Thinking about what came after Christmas, she felt a shock of pure fear. What if they failed? Bru, with his first taste of love and happiness since his father had left, was twice as vulnerable as when he'd come to Florida. It would really be bad if he couldn't hope to live with his dad.

"Stop worrying," Alec said, uncannily aware of her thoughts. "We're going to win. I have a definite feeling that from now on, everything will go right for us."

13

"YOU TOLD ME," Gail mumbled groggily, "that you wakened with the first faint light." She twisted a little to give the warm, exploring hand a bit more freedom. "The first faint light isn't here yet. Go to sleep."

"I am asleep. Stop interfering with my dream."

Her smile went unseen in the darkness before dawn. It was cold in her little room, but under the covers Alec radiated warmth. His husky whisper warmed her ear; his stroking hand coaxed her relaxed body into a delicious feeling of boneless contentment, as if she floated in a tropical sea. She turned a little more and stretched, offering herself to his hand, closing her eyes and letting herself drift into desire.

"Gail . . . I'm not waking you too early, am I?"

A bubble of laughter rose in her throat. "You're not waking me at all. I'm just part of your dream." She could feel his rising passion in his trembling hand, the heat and hardness pressing against her thigh. Soon his hand would know what she already knew, that her secret recesses were begging for him, beginning to ache with exquisite need.

"You're not part of my dream," he whispered. "You're all of it. Make it come true."

She sighed and gave in, turning toward him and beginning to caress his body, which she now knew so well, loved so well. She was startled a moment later when he arched upward and dragged her beneath him, taking her with a gentle desperation.

"Gail . . . angel. If only I could be *sure* of you. . . ."

IT WAS EIGHT A.M. Gail had an appointment at nine, but she was still in her robe, sitting in the living room and dreamily watching Alec over the rim of her coffee cup. Unshaven, wearing his trousers and a wrinkled shirt, his dark gold curls in disorder, he lounged in the chair opposite her with a look of supreme contentment.

"Either this is the best coffee I've ever tasted," he said, "or I feel so great because I'm with you. Since I made the coffee, it has to be you. From now on we spend the nights together. No more of those midnight treks—" He stopped, looked toward the door, then back at Gail, who was suddenly frozen in her chair. "Did someone knock?"

"Yes," Gail whispered, blood rising in her cheeks. "It's Mrs. Langford. She always knocks like that—just a touch you can barely hear. You'd better . . ."

Alec had already slipped out into the hall and into the bedroom, out of sight. Gail swallowed and got up, tightening the sash of her robe. She managed a smile as she opened the door.

"Good morning."

"Here," Mrs. Langford said, thrusting a bowl into Gail's hands. "That's the bowl I use for Puppy, and you may as well have it." Her usually pleasant old face was pale, and her mouth quivered in spite of her obvious effort to look dignified. She drew herself up and went on shakily.

"I just hate to do this, Gail, but you'll have to leave. A rule is a rule, and I won't play favorites. I'll give you a week to find another place."

Speechless, Gail took the bowl, nodded and finally got out a few words. "I wouldn't ask you to play favorites, Mrs. Langford. But your rule isn't a very realistic one these days."

"Of course it isn't. I lose a lot of tenants. But somebody has to uphold the old values, so I do. It's very wearing for an elderly person. I'm up half the night listening for people leaving." She looked past Gail into the living room. "I don't suppose you'll want to sell any of that furniture. I've always admired those chairs."

"No," Gail said gently. "I expect I'll need it all."

"All right. As I said, I'm sorry." The old woman turned away, then looked back. "At least you didn't try to lie, Gail. I respect you for that."

"Thank you," Gail replied, suddenly amused. "I don't lie. That's one of the values I uphold." She shut the door and turned to Alec in the hall, coming toward her.

"I could kick myself," he said. "This is all my fault. You told me, but I didn't believe it until now. When in God's name does that old woman sleep?"

Gail had to laugh. "During the day, I guess. During the night she upholds the old values. Don't worry about it, Alec. I really don't mind."

"I'll help," he said, and put his arms around her, his cheek bristly against hers. "Moving is a chore. But we've got a week. By then I'll have talked you into marrying me, and we won't have a problem. You can just move in."

Gail drew away, feeling a flash of resentment. He was trying to make her eviction into a reason for her to forget her true convictions and sign that damnable paper. "We have no problem now," she said coolly. "I'll simply store my furniture and move in with my parents until I can find a place."

Alec stood immobile, staring at her. Just knowing she would have to move had boosted his confidence and his hopes. It was like a sign, but still Gail had refused. And meant it.

"You're never going to marry me, are you?" he asked quietly, and the disappointment in his voice touched her heart. She reached up to stroke his unshaven cheek, regret darkening her eyes. "No, Alec, I'm not. And you know why. But I love you. Isn't that enough?"

He turned and walked out, leaving his coat and top-coat behind, and headed for his own house. Somehow he had been sure that the next time they'd discussed marriage she'd give in. Because of Bru, because of her parents and because of the growing feeling between them. He had changed; he had grown to depend on her more every day. But she hadn't changed at all! She was so stubborn. Well, she'd find out he was, too. He went in the back door and ran up the stairs angrily. He'd help her move; he'd promised that. But afterward he'd stay away until she came to him with compromise on her mind.

Maybe it's for the best, Gail thought. She needed to leave this neighborhood. Maybe this town. Alec's problems would resolve themselves in one way or another, and he needed a chance to make a new life—with the right woman. Not one who demanded what he couldn't give.

As she dressed, then hurriedly made the rumpled bed, her throat was tight. Waking in his arms had felt wonderful—as if she were surrounded by love. She was suddenly profoundly grateful to old Mrs. Langford.

The feeling she'd had upon waking could be habit-forming, and she had her own values to uphold.

ON CHRISTMAS EVE Gail was finally settled in the guest room at the Winslow house. Her own room, the one in the back, which she had occupied from her childhood until leaving home, was Bru's room now. She didn't mind. She liked knowing he woke up to the sight of the big oak tree outside the window, the inviting stretch of lawn and woods that waited for his running feet.

"I'm glad you're here," Virginia said as they finished decorating the tree. "I mean living here right now. Your father and I will need you and Alec to cheer us up. It'll be like a morgue around here once they take Bru away next week."

"I know." Gail kept her eyes on the box of old ornaments she was sifting through. There was no use in upsetting Virginia further; she would wait until the holidays were over to tell her that she and Alec were also over. Except for helping her move, as he had promised to do, Alec hadn't been alone with her since that morning Mrs. Langford had told her to leave. She knew it was at least partly because she'd refused him again.

He was tired, Gail thought now, hanging another ornament on the tree. Tired of being turned down. Or maybe just tired of arguing with her. When they were with her parents and Bru, he acted as he always had, but after Bru left Alec would stop coming, and she'd have to tell her parents why.

"Alec is going to spend the night here tonight," Virginia said conversationally, then laughed as Gail turned and gave her an astonished stare. "I know, the bedrooms are full. He'll sleep on the couch in your father's study. Bru wanted him here on Christmas morning."

"That couch is too short for him."

Virginia shrugged. "One night won't hurt. Or you can trade places with him. The couch isn't too short for you." She stood back and flung the last handful of tinsel as high as she could on the laden tree, wiped her hands and looked at Gail critically. "Of course, it would be a lot simpler if you'd marry the man. But until you do, don't expect me to put the two of you in one bed. What you do in your own houses is one thing, but—"

"I don't expect that," Gail broke in hastily. "I—I'm perfectly satisfied with your arrangements. In fact, I prefer them. Don't give it another thought."

"Now wait a minute. When you don't argue it makes me nervous. I don't want any sneaky bed hopping, either."

"Mother!"

"Let's go finish dinner," Virginia said briskly. "Dave and Bru and Alec will be coming in here like a pack of starving wolves. And don't look at me like that. I had to be sure you knew that the rules of this house haven't changed."

The scent of pine and the drifting aroma of mince pie filled the house as evening came on. It was the custom at the Winslow house to have the celebratory dinner on Christmas Eve, followed by a buffet on Christmas. Outside, the huge, rainbow waterfalls of colored lights winked and sparkled and changed the lawn and house into a glowing fairyland.

Driving toward the house in fast-growing darkness, Alec was tired and glum. He hadn't been sleeping well, and he couldn't believe how much he missed Gail. He wasn't looking forward to the stay at the Winslow's house, but he couldn't disappoint Bru. Now the glow surrounding the house was a mockery, reminding him that others were providing this warmth and joy for Bru, that within a few days Hewlett would be taking his son away. On top of that he'd talked to his lawyer again, and the lawyer, who had now investigated thoroughly, had told him he didn't have a ghost of a chance against Hewlett. Alec believe it, because he hadn't been able to think of anything himself. For the first time in his life, Alec Morgan felt like a loser.

Gail saw his feelings on his face as he came in the door. His flat cheeks were lined with fatigue; his hazel eyes were dull and lifeless. He glanced at her, then looked away as he removed his coat. She took the coat from him and hung it on the coat rack, knowing he was in the depths of despair, feeling suddenly seized with love and guilt. Right now Alec really needed someone who cared, and she hadn't been there for him at all. She turned back and put her arms around him.

"Merry Christmas," she said, and kissed him, feeling his arms close around her hard, feeling the ice crack away from her own guarded heart. His lips were cold from the outside air, but hungry, starving, as they closed strongly over her warm and willing mouth.

"Oh, Lord," he whispered, "how I've missed you, angel. I should have known—"

A door slammed behind them down the hall. "Dad! Hey, Grandma, Dad is here!"

Gail stepped back just in time to get out of the way of Bru's flying leap at Alec. She watched as Alec hugged his son; then she left them together and went to help Virginia in the kitchen. Only a few days more.

"Stop that," Virginia said, noting Gail's gloomy face. "We'll all sit down and bawl once Bru is gone, but right now we're going to give him—in fact, we're going to give all of us—a wonderful time to remember."

"Yes," Gail said. "You're right. Absolutely right. Tell me where to start." She grabbed up the dishes her mother indicated and began carrying them in. She felt awful. Her mother was right and she was wrong. Absolutely wrong. She should never have kissed Alec tonight, never have let her feelings rule her again. There was no room for compromise between them, no way she could agree to sign that blamed paper, no way he could give her the love and trust she had to have. Alec must have realized that when he'd stopped seeing her, and now she'd started it all over again. She looked up as the dining-room door opened and Alec came in. Their eyes met across the shining table and there it was—that look she could never explain, that recognition, that feeling that she was looking into the other side of herself.

"We have to talk, Gail."

She kept walking around the table, setting the plates down with trembling hands. "Not now. This is Bru's time. We—we'll talk later. Maybe when it's all over."

He came closer, watching as she put down the last plate. Then he took her hands and turned her to face him. "Listen. This won't take long to say, and you can be thinking about it. We'll sit down together with that agreement and go over it word by word. You can tell me exactly how you want it changed, and I'll—"

"No."

He drew in a deep breath. "Dammit, Gail, you could let me finish. You don't have to answer now, just think about it. I'll bring you one of the copies so you can study it. Please don't say no yet."

She kept on looking at him, at the pleading in his hazel eyes, the uncertainty and hope. Like Bru he needed to be happy, at least for a while. He needed *her* until it was over. Time enough then to face the facts. "All right," she said finally. "Bring it. But remember, I'm not promising anything."

He let out his breath in a whoosh of relief and pulled her into his arms, holding her close, his heart pounding against her breasts. "Wonderful! That's all I need. I can prove to you it'll work like a charm...."

"If you two lovebirds will cooperate," Virginia said from the kitchen door, "we may get through dinner in time to take Bru to the Christmas Eve pageant at the church."

AT MIDNIGHT, with Bru tucked in and asleep in his room, they brought out the eggnog and drank it, while piling the presents around the tree. When they were finished the bottom limbs were hidden by colorful packages in various shapes and sizes and by a ribbon-bedecked bicycle Dave brought in from its hiding place in the woodworking shop.

"So," Virginia said happily, running slender fingers through her dark, silver-streaked hair. "Maybe the bike is silly when Bru has so little time to enjoy it, but if he can't take it with him we'll store it until summer. It'll be one more thing for him to look forward to."

"The same with the computer and the trains," Alec said, waving his glass at two big boxes. "But once my house is finished I can solve your storage problems. Everything looks great, Ginny. I can never thank you two enough for what you've done for Bru."

Virginia grinned at him. "For Bru? More like for Ginny and Dave. This is the best Christmas we've had since Gail grew up." She turned and put an arm around Dave's waist. "Come along, love. I'm a bit tiddly, and these are late hours for us. Gail and Alec can finish the details and then go to bed."

"What a wonderful thought," Alec said as the door closed behind them. "Let's hurry those details."

Gail stared at the bottom of her empty glass, feeling slightly embarrassed. "Like Mrs. Langford, my mother upholds the old values. The rules in this house haven't been changed in forty years. In other words, she definitely did not mean we should go to bed together."

"Somehow," Alec said slowly, "I'm not surprised."

Gail sighed. "Good. Now that we've got that out of the way, you can have my bed and I'll take the couch down here. It's just right for me, but too short for you." She glanced up at Alec and found him looking at her with so much warmth and happiness that her throat constricted. She had wanted to keep things light, but he kept forcing her to be serious. "Stop thinking what you're thinking," she added in a breathy whisper. "You're inciting a rebellion. . . ."

"How can you say that?" He took her glass and placed it with his beneath the tree. Then he put his arms around her and pushed her flat on the worn Oriental rug her mother had had from the Year One and kissed her until she couldn't breathe. She caught at his wandering hand and held it, felt the rush and sweep of desire blotting out thought, and moaned helplessly.

"Oh, Alec . . . we shouldn't. . . ."

"We aren't." Husky-voiced and heated, he lifted himself and then her, scrambling to his feet and holding her tight. "We *won't*." Their bodies were welded together; their mouths moved over each others' faces in small, frenzied caresses, and then Alec was drawing away, breathing deeply. "We didn't. See? Go to bed before I change my mind."

Gail laughed, a soft, broken sound. "You take the bed, I'll sleep down here. My room's at the head of the stairs."

"No. Dave brought me a pillow and a blanket and gave me the use of his study. I'll be fine. Go, angel. Now."

She went, and in some calm corner of her mind she wondered if her mother had planned all this just to make her wish she had married Alec. Because she did.

It was hard to get to sleep, even full of eggnog, and after she did manage to drop off it seemed only a few minutes before she heard the familiar creak of her old bedroom door and realized Bru was on his way downstairs.

It was still dark, of course. But if it was true that the night was darkest just before dawn, it wouldn't be dark long. But Bru would wake Alec—and Alec had looked exhausted. She flung on her woolly robe and stuck her feet in slippers, went out and ran down the dimly lighted stairs, seeing from the glow in the living room that Bru had turned on the tree lights.

She went on, and in spite of her fatigue she felt herself smiling. It had been a long time, but not so long that she had forgotten how it felt to be a child at Christmas. In a moment there would be the sounds of paper tearing, the half-muffled yelps of joy, the scrambling for another package.

But there wasn't. Coming silently to the door, she saw Bru kneeling on the floor in front of the lighted tree, quiet and motionless. His pajamas revealed that he was bony and still too thin; his solemn young face was lifted to the wonder of the treetop angel and the lights. He looked... Gail drew in a sharp breath and felt her heart squeeze hard. He looked so sad.

"Merry Christmas," she whispered, and went in, aching to touch him, to take him in her arms, knowing he'd probably hate it. Instead she dropped down beside him and smiled.

"So, what do you think?"

In answer he turned and put his arms around her, pushing his face into her shoulder, holding on tight. "Why can't I stay, Gail? L-look at all the presents for me—everybody must l-like me a l-little."

She hugged him, rocking back and forth, swallowing tears. "Nobody likes you a little," she managed finally. "Everybody loves you a lot. We all want you to stay, Bru. We'd do anything to keep you here with us. But your mother wants you with her until school is over. Then...*then*, Bru, you come back here, and we'll have the biggest party you've ever had."

He pulled away and looked at her doubtfully. "Marian said when Dad got a girlfriend he wouldn't want me around anymore."

So that was it. Gail smiled and pushed her hair out of her eyes again. "Looks like she was mistaken, doesn't it?"

"I guess so." The green eyes regarded her steadily. "She said the girlfriend wouldn't like it, either. She'd think I was in the way. Am I?"

Careful. Don't rush into this. Gail drew her knees up and rested her arms on them, thinking. "Let's see," she said at last. "Just who might be in the way around here. First—do you want to be your dad's girlfriend?"

"Of course not," Bru said, suddenly indignant. "I'm not a *girl*."

"True," Gail said, nodding. "So you can't be in my way. And I don't want to be your dad's little boy, so I'm not in your way. Well, what do you know? I guess nobody's in the way."

Bru sat back and laughed. "That's silly, Gail, you know that? You couldn't be a boy."

"Thank heaven for that," Alec said behind them, and came forward, yawning, half-dressed, wrapped in a blanket. He sat down on the other side of Bru and tousled his hair. "Merry Christmas, you night owls. Do you know what time it is?"

Gail met his eyes and smiled weakly. Bristly bearded, his cheeks creased from the pillow, Alec was warm and sleepy and irresistible. "I'm afraid to ask."

"Barely five o'clock. It'll be a good two hours before it's light enough to ride a bike." He looked at Bru's suddenly pleading green eyes and grinned. "However, I happen to know there are a few other things you might like around here. Dive in." He leaned back on his elbows and laughed as Bru began plundering the pile of packages, ripping off paper.

"I'll make coffee," Gail said, getting to her feet. "And some hot chocolate for Bru."

"Great," Alec said, smiling up her. "I'll need it. But then you get back to bed and rest. I'll stay up."

Pausing in mid rip, Bru looked around. "Hey, wait a minute, now. Don't you go sending Gail off to bed. I want her in on this, too."

14

"THERE ARE FEW perfect days," Virginia said from the doorway. "But I think we've just lived through one. I peeked in at Bru. He's sound asleep." She came into the living room and sank down on the love seat with Dave, smiling at Gail and Alec, sitting opposite. "And why not? He must be exhausted. Every time I looked up he was shooting past the window on that bike. More dessert? There's one whole pecan pie left."

They looked at one another and laughed. "One more bite," Gail said, "and my perfect day would be ruined. What I need is a long walk."

"Take the flashlight on the hall table," Dave said. "There's no moon."

"We won't need it, thanks," Gail said, standing and stretching. "We'll be walking along the seawall, and it's very well lighted." She smiled at Alec as he rose and brought her coat. "You go ahead," she said to him, "and I'll follow in my car. I'll need it for work tomorrow."

"But . . ." Virginia was confused. "Aren't you coming back home?"

"Certainly I am." Gail leaned over and kissed her mother's cheek, then Dave's. "Tomorrow night. See you then."

Dave followed them out to the entrance and spoke to Alec. "Ginny said you planned to take Bru home tonight, but she asked to keep him for the rest of the week. That suits me, too, but I want to be prepared. When do you expect Hewlett and the Sommers to show up? Soon?"

"I hope not. I assume they'll wait until after New Year's, but I really don't know." Alec's relaxed face hardened at the thought; his brows drew together. "My hands are tied, Dave. I know in my bones that it's wrong for Bru to go back, but nothing can be done until we find some proof of neglect. My lawyer has located a good private investigator, who will be on the case from now on—we'll get Hewlett, but it will take time."

"And cause trouble for Bru," Dave said savagely. "You can count on one thing—I won't let them have him if they come here without you. Damn it all, I just wish there were something we could do."

"You've done plenty," Alec said. "You and Ginny have helped give him a security he's never had, and he knows he'll be coming back to it." He clapped Dave on the shoulder. "Be warned—you've probably gotten yourself a lifetime job."

Outside, Alec and Gail went down the steps into the multicolored glow of winking lights and paused to breathe in the cold, piney air. Above the glow, stars shone like diamonds in a black and distant sky. Pulling her close, Alec kissed her lightly, his mouth warm on her cold face.

"A wonderful Christmas, darling."

"Yes." She rested her forehead on his shoulder, her arms still around his waist, and was quiet. "Bru really wants to stay here," she said finally. "Before you got up this morning he—well, he spoke about it. I hope he understands how hard you're trying to fix it so he can come back for good."

"I talked to him today," Alec said. "He knows. But he's very quiet. It's just hard for him to wait." He drew her toward her car and opened the door. "You go first, angel. It's easier to keep an eye on you that way."

All he meant by that, Gail thought as she drove away, was that if anything happened—a flat tire, for instance—he'd be handy. But the way it sounded was the way Alec really felt. Somehow, deep inside, he really believed he had to keep an eye on her. He couldn't trust her not to leave him, not to let him down. And he was right. That was exactly what she was going to do when this was over. She would leave him. Not because she was faithless—only because he couldn't trust enough to love.

Glancing in the rearview mirror, she saw his car swing out from the driveway and follow. When he'd asked her to go home with him for the night she hadn't hesitated. Maybe she should have, but she kept thinking of how it must be for him to know that in spite of all he was doing he was about to lose Bru again. Besides, to be truthful, she couldn't say no to her own desire. This might be her last chance to dream that beautiful, unattainable dream of real love that haunted her still.

Pulling in beside her behind his house, Alec got out, came to her where she stood by her car and took her arm, his long fingers cool and tense. "Still want that walk?"

She looked up at his shadowed face and smiled. "Yes. A fresh sea breeze may be exactly what I need for my case of megrims. Do you mind?"

He laughed and turned her to the brick-paved alley that led up toward the fort. Dim, eerily lighted by the glow from lamps behind curtained windows, the alley was narrow and swept by a hard northeast wind. Huddled together and shivering, warm only where they touched, they pushed on to the Avenida Menendez and the seawall.

Mostly they walked in silence, listening to the wash and swirl of unseen waves. Overhead, the seawall lights, brilliant in the black night, shone, their reflections glittering on the black, restless water of Mantanzas Bay.

Lost in private thoughts they bumped awkwardly, separated, paused and laughed. Then he shortened his stride and she lengthened hers until they matched, looking at each other and still laughing, breathing in the sharp tang of salt, blinking away tears from the cold wind. Turning to go back, Alec put an arm around her and led her across the Avenida, down the street past the cathedral to the protected inner streets. There they could swing along while the wind battered the treetops above them.

"Feel better?" Hugging her to him, Alec smiled down into her eyes. "Breeze fresh enough?"

She chuckled, ducking her head, liking his teasing. The wind had doubled in strength while they walked. "You'd better hope it won't swing to the northwest, darling. If it does, your roses will freeze."

"In that case I hope it won't. I like those roses." He stopped her in the trembling shadow of a huge, windwhipped tree and held her close. "Remember the first time we kissed, angel? Full of wine, we were, together in a warm, rose-scented night. . . ."

He was kissing her again, while the cold wind tossed her hair like a dark red banner. It was just as thrilling as the first time. No, it was better. She clung to him, suddenly weak. "Take me home, Alec. Make love to me."

IN GAIL'S SECRET FANTASY their love would live forever. In the quiet, subdued luxury of Alec's bedroom, with the wild wind shut out, she gave herself to him in sensuous surrender, as if there had been no yesterday, as if there would be no tomorrow. He responded by being so tender and caring that afterward, lying stunned and quivering from the giant waves of pleasure he brought her, tears came to her eyes. He kissed her eyes shut and licked the tears from her cheeks with a warm tongue.

"What is making you sad, my darling?"

"Have you never heard of happy tears?"

He laughed, and she laughed with him, sorry for her small deception, but unable to tell him of the dark sadness that lurked just outside the bright circle of their lovemaking. It was impossible for her to forget that tonight, or any of the nights coming soon, could be the last.

Close and warm in the middle of the wide bed they talked, ignoring the hour, going over the day and Bru's pleasure in his presents, Dave's delight in the complicated electric trains, Ginny's thrilled satisfaction with everything.

"Except her daughter," Gail amended ruefully. "Mom's such a great wife and mother, contented and happy to stay at home and look after Dad. I suppose she wonders where she got me."

Alec grinned. "A mix-up in the nursery ward? Never mind, she'll be fine once we marry and have more children."

"There you go again, taking me for granted."

"No, I'm not. It's just that I know we can reach a compromise on that agreement once you settle down long enough to go over it with me."

Gail turned, putting an arm across his chest, her face in the curve of his neck. She was silent, even though she could feel that Alec was waiting, wanting her to say something. Hoping, she thought, that what she'd say would be encouraging. Instead she wriggled closer and began a subtle caressing that she knew from experience would drive him pleasantly crazy. He rolled, capturing her beneath him, cupping the sides of her head and staring down into her half-closed eyes.

"Believe me, angel. I mean it. All you're going to have to do is tell me what you want in that agreement, and it'll be that way."

Her eyelids drooped farther, until her lashes rested on her cheeks. The corners of her mouth turned up in a slow smile. "How can I believe you? Just now I was *showing* you what I wanted and you simply ignored me...."

He laughed and gave up, his mouth stopping her teasing.

THEY WOKE LATE to the battering of wind and torrential rains against the east windows. The clock said a quarter to ten, but the winter storm had blotted out the sun and left nothing but dim gray light. Later, showered and dressed and making coffee, Gail watched the wet, tossing tops of palms across the street and turned to look at Alec, lounging against the counter beside her.

"I have only one appointment today, and that's with a builder. He won't mind waiting. I think I'll cancel it and spend some time with Bru this afternoon."

"With Bru and me," Alec said, sounding smug. "I told Penny last week I'd take emergencies only from Christmas through New Year's."

He grinned and Gail grinned back. "But that's wonderful. We've got a vacation." She opened the refrigerator and looked in. "Plenty for brunch, and by noon the rain will stop. . . ."

"How do you know that?"

"I'm taking it for granted," she said, getting out orange juice. "It started before seven o'clock, and my grandfather always said rain that starts before seven stops before eleven."

"It's ten-thirty now."

"Well, then," she went on, pouring juice. "It should begin to slacken off. Or—" she handed him a glass "—my guess is wrong and it started after seven." She looked toward the windows and pointed. Alec swung around and straightened. Rain still dropped in silver sheets from the roof, but the sky above had brightened, and a watery sunlight shone on the trees. They were still laughing at her accurate forecast, when the telephone rang.

"Maybe I bragged too soon," Alec said, heading for the phone. "That's probably Penny now, and if she's phoning, it has to be an emergency."

Pushing down a sudden sense of impending doom, Gail turned back and began taking out ingredients for a quiche. She decided she was borrowing trouble. Emergencies were common in a doctor's life. She whirled as Alec spoke, his voice strained and harsh.

"I thought you intended to wait until after New Year's, Hewlett."

Gail saw Alec's powerful shoulders slump. His face fell into unfamiliar, defeated lines as he listened.

"I could kill him!" she said vehemently as, after a few more words, Alec put down the phone. "I could! What right has he to separate a father from his son just so a—a Hewlett can win?"

Alec looked at her in surprise. Her face was scarlet, her eyes brilliant with rage. When he put his arms around her he could feel her trembling tension. He held her, smoothing her hair. "You really are angry," he said wonderingly. "Don't be, darling. There's nothing we can do."

She leaned against him, trying to control herself. "But he has sons of his own! He's proud of them. H-he said they were good men." Her voice rose. "Does he think *he's* a good man, taking your son away from you?"

"Shh," Alec murmured. "Calm down, angel. He doesn't look at it that way. He's probably doing what he thinks is his duty, returning a runaway boy to his mother. Remember, legally he's right."

Gail leaned back and looked up at him, her futile anger beginning to subside. "I suppose he is. I just wish he could see that in this case he's morally wrong."

Alec smiled, his hazel eyes warm and indulgent as he let her go. "Remember, we're not giving up, darling. We'll get our evidence, and when we do we'll get Bru." He reached out and tipped her face up, beginning to grin. "I hope you never get that angry with me, tigress." He laughed softly as she flushed, this time with embarrassment. "I'm not criticizing, though. It's wonderful that you care."

"You knew I did," Gail said, turning back to her preparations. "We all care." It seemed necessary to drag her parents in, though she didn't know why. Stirring nervously, she added, "I guessed from what I heard you say, they're coming to get him before New Year's."

"They're coming to get him this afternoon."

"Alec!" She whirled around and sank down on the kitchen stool, staring at him. "They're taking him tonight? How can they, with no warning? We need time . . . we have to pack his clothes, his presents . . . we need to—to tell him."

"He knows," Alec said, looking suddenly bleak. "We talked, remember? He knows I'm going to be fighting to have him live with me. He knows it will take time. He knows he's going to have to go back. He knows everything except when they're picking him up. He has plenty of clothes up north, and we can send what he leaves behind. As for when he has to leave here, maybe it's better he doesn't know, and can't be counting the hours."

"When will they be here?"

"There's no way to tell. Hewlett said they may be late. They had a miserable crossing from the Bahamas over to the mainland in rain and wind and Louisa was frightened and upset. They'll wait until she's calm enough to ride in the car. But Hewlett said they would definitely be up here by this evening."

"I see." Gail stared at her hands, feeling helpless. "I guess," she said finally, "that after we eat we should drive out to my folks' place so you can be with Bru. I'll leave it to you to break the news to all three of them."

Alec put an arm around her and gave her a reassuring squeeze. "I know. It's no fun to carry bad news. But we'll all make it, and next year will be different."

Alec was already different, Gail thought later, sliding the quiche in the oven. He had changed a lot. He had lost that cynical look, that deep bitterness that used to surface once in a while, and he seemed even more sensitive to and perceptive of other peoples' feelings. A wonderful father, and a marvelous lover. For a moment she pictured the future—a future she'd hidden away—and looked at it squarely. Taking Alec out of that picture left an enormous void. He'd feel it, too, she realized suddenly; he'd be alone again, closed up once more in his shell, cold and hard. Maybe it would be worth it to at least try it his way.

She straightened and looked over at him as he stood at the big windows, staring out at the clearing sky. She was afraid that if she married him knowing he couldn't trust her, after a while her own love and faith would shrivel and die. It was too much to risk. But how in the world could they manage to stay away from each other? They had tried it twice now, but at the first chance they snapped back together as if magnetized.

"It's crazy to let one phone call ruin a whole day," Alec said, sitting down to eat. "We may have most of an afternoon—let's use it. We can take Bru and inspect the house." His gaze came up to Gail's face and his eyes crinkled as he smiled. "It's not quite ready for you to start planning the decor, but it's taking shape."

"Fine," Gail said casually, handing him a bowl of fruit and a knife for the quiche. "Bru enjoys making plans. It makes the summer real for him. We'll take Puppy and tramp around in the woods." She was trying hard to avoid thinking about Bru leaving, and now she fastened her mind on the Dobie and the problem of finding an apartment where she would be allowed to have him with her. Of course her parents would keep him as long as necessary, but she wanted his company. Except, she thought, for when Bru came back....

"Be sure to tell Bru that Puppy can stay with him when he comes back next summer. You'll be living out by the lake then, and I won't mind a bit. They really like each other."

Alec turned his head sharply and stared at her. "I thought that *we'd* be living out there by then, and that included Puppy."

It had been dumb to make any remark about the future at this point, and that one, Gail realized, had been particularly stupid. Saying it had made it very plain that she had no intention of living with Alec, married or unmarried. Not looking at him, she made a small, helpless gesture with one hand.

"Who knows what can happen by then?" she asked, feeling like a coward. "I just want to be sure Bru doesn't worry...." She stopped talking as Alec leaned back and put down his fork. The sun had begun to shine brightly and the light from the window accented the grim lines of his face.

"You promised to go over that agreement with me, Gail. Are you reneging on that promise?"

"I didn't promise," Gail said shakily. "I carefully told you to remember I wasn't making any promises. But I did say to bring me a copy, and . . . and so I'll go over the damn thing if that's what you want. But it's a waste of time, because it's not going to make any difference. Don't you see, Alec? That's not what the argument is about. As far as the agreement is concerned, I don't think it's unfair."

His brows shot up. "Good! Then you can give it to your attorney tomorrow and by next week we'll be married."

Gail stared down at her untouched plate. He was pushing again. He knew how she felt and he chose to ignore it. "Let's drop it, Alec. We've enough to worry about today, haven't we?"

"But this is part of it all," Alec said, reaching across the table and taking her hand. "I was hoping to cheer up Bru before he left by telling him that when he came back he'd have both of us as parents. . . ."

Gail gasped and snatched her hand away from him. "You—you rat! Don't you *dare* tell him that! What a lousy trick, trying to play on my sympathy for Bru! Besides, what makes you think he even wants a stepmother? He certainly didn't when you brought it up before."

"He does now," Alec said stiffly. "He told me so last night. Some rambling account about how we'd all be happy in the new house because nobody would be in the way. I suppose because the house is big."

She could have told him that wasn't what Bru meant, but she didn't. Glancing at him, she saw that he was hurt and holding down anger.

"Please," she said, instead. "Let's not think of our own differences. Bru has the real problem. Let's think of him."

Alec took a deep breath and picked up the coffee-pot, pouring two cups of coffee before he spoke. "All right," he said finally, putting down the pot. "And I'm sorry. I admit I was using Bru to push you my way, and it really was a lousy trick. I'm ashamed of myself."

Gail glanced up at him, her eyes softening. "Apology accepted. It wasn't like you, Alec."

He gave her a half cocky, half rueful grin. "How do you know what a man is like when he's desperate?"

15

COMING DOWN the front steps, Virginia waved and smiled, first at Gail in her station wagon, then at Alec, pulling in behind her.

"Thank heaven," Virginia caroled. "You'll both be here for dinner. We've got to get rid of that pie—" She stopped suddenly, staring at Gail. "What's wrong? You look terrible."

"Thanks, Mom," Gail said shortly, climbing out. "I needed that. Where's Bru?"

Virginia's bright face dimmed. "Now wait a minute. I know that expression, Gail. Answer my question."

Gail sighed. She heard Alec's car door close, his footsteps behind her, then felt his arm around her shoulders. Looking up at him, she said, "I guess I'm not very good at hiding my feelings. The Grand Inquisitor here wants to know what's wrong."

Alec swung an arm across Virginia's shoulders, too, and turned them both toward the house. "Nothing new, Ginny. But Bru's leaving today, not next week. Hewlett is coming to pick him up. You tell Dave, but leave it to me, please, to tell Bru."

Virginia nodded. "For once," she said weakly, "I'm sorry I asked. If you want to tell him now, he's in the living room. He and Dave are playing with the trains."

Alec hesitated as they got to the door, then shook his head. "No. I'm not looking forward to telling him, and there's no hurry. Why ruin his whole afternoon?"

"You're right," Virginia agreed, sniffling. "Let him enjoy himself while he can."

"Somehow," Gail said thoughtfully, "I think he could handle it now just as well as later. But, then, what difference does it make when he handles it as long as he knows they're coming before they get here?"

Virginia looked at her blankly. "In order to answer you I'd have to understand the question. Would you care to repeat it?"

"Dad! You guys come see the train tunnel Grandpa made out of an old mailbox!"

Standing in the living room doorway with the Christmas tree behind him, Bru radiated excitement. Sudden sympathy squeezed Gail's heart as they all turned to follow him back into the room. Why spoil a minute of his happiness? He'd find out soon enough.

"WHEN HE COMES IN, I'll tell him," Alec said at four o'clock. "I'm not going to go out there and drag him off his bike for news like that."

"I'll go up and pack a small bag," Virginia said dismally, and started for the stairs. "He won't need much on the trip."

"I'll help," Dave said, rising. "I want to make sure the carving of the Doberman is wrapped right."

For the past hour Gail had felt increasingly nervous. It seemed risky to wait so long before telling Bru. Of course he knew he was going to have to leave, but the last few days he thought he'd have were important to him. She turned from the window where she had been watching for Bru and came back to the center of the room, glancing at Alec.

"I'll get him," she said. "I'd like a breath of air myself."

Sprawled in a corner of the couch, Alec looked at her broodingly. "I hate this," he said. "But it's time, I guess. Send him in here."

She nodded and left, going through the hall and taking a sweater from the coat rack. Putting it on, she went outside and down the steps, shivering in the rapidly cooling air. The big live oaks in the yard, still covered with strings of colored bulbs, looked faded and dreary with the lights off. Dead leaves littered the lawn and sifted across the walk. Gail shivered again, depressed, and walked out to the road, looking both ways for a boy on a bike and a large black dog.

To the north, toward the highway, she spotted a car, then Bru on his bike, pedaling along on the shoulder of the road, keeping out of the way. Puppy loped beside him.

Relaxing, Gail leaned on the mailbox and waited. She smiled slightly as the car slowed to a crawl behind Bru. She was always supercareful herself when a child on a bike showed up ahead. You never knew what they'd do.... She gasped and straightened, staring as Bru, pedaling fast, angled his bike off the road into high, tough grass and weeds, fell over and scrambled back up. He took off, leaving the bike and running for the woods, with Puppy right behind him. *Why?* Her gaze shot back to the car.

"Sommers," she breathed. "Oh, no. Please no." But it was. Dick Sommers, heavy and red faced, was leaving the open door of the stopped car, striding into the field. He gestured and called to Bru's small, fleeing figure, his words indistinguishable.

They had waited too long to tell Bru. Her shoulders sagging, Gail started walking toward the car. Somehow she'd have to get Bru to come back, smooth things over and bring them all to the house. From here she could see two others in the back of the car, and Dick moving farther and farther toward the woods, still yelling and, from the sound of it, getting madder by the minute.

Picking up her pace, Gail gave a disgusted sigh. Couldn't Dick see his angry yelling wasn't bringing Bru back? Suddenly she gasped again and began to run, awkwardly at first, then her long legs reaching, flying. At last Dick's yelling and chasing were having an effect. They were bringing the Dobie at full gallop, head down, ears flat, lips curled in a white-toothed snarl.

"Stand still!" Gail screamed, breathless. "Stand *still*, Dick! No, Puppy! Oh, Lord, *no!*"

Sommers had seen the danger. Whether he had heard Gail or not she couldn't know, but he had turned and started running as hard as he could for the car. The Dobie caught up in a blur of speed, launched his ninety pounds of fury at Dick's back and brought him crashing down. Dancing around him, growling ferociously, Puppy snapped his long jaws at Dick's head and shoulders, threatening, terrorizing, ready to nail him if he moved.

Plunging through the high weeds, Gail flung herself between them and pushed the dog away, trying to catch her breath, trying to get words out.

"Bru," she managed finally, pushing at the Dobie's shoulder. "Go find Bru!"

Puppy raised his head, looked at her and whirled, racing toward the woods. Trembling, aware that Sommers was silent and motionless but breathing, Gail pushed away from his prone body and sat back, glancing up as Roger Hewlett and Louisa Sommers came hurriedly toward her.

"You'd better go on to the house and call for an ambulance," she said as they neared. "Dick seems to be unconscious."

Louisa stopped, uttered a little scream and hid her face behind her hands. "Is there a lot of blood, Roger? I can't stand the sight of blood."

"I don't see any," Roger replied calmly. "I think he's fainted. He's always been easily frightened."

"Now, Roger," Louisa said, injured. "You know Dick has a bad heart. This could be a heart attack." She looked suddenly upset by the thought. "What do you think, Mrs. Sheridan?"

Gail stood up, brushing dry leaves and clinging grass from her clothes. Her mind was on Bru, hiding in the woods with Puppy, afraid to come out. She didn't really care what was wrong with Dick Sommers.

"What I think," she said to Louisa, "is that he's too heavy for us to move and what we need is an ambulance. I'll go call one."

"I'll go with you," Louisa said immediately. "Roger can stay with Dick, in case he begins bleeding."

"An ambulance is an unnecessary expense," Roger said coldly. "And anyway, here comes Morgan. He's a doctor. Let him take a look at Dick. Then if he has to go to the hospital we can take him there in the car."

Gail turned to see Alec running toward them, with Dave behind him, losing ground but coming on. At her feet, Dick Sommers groaned and moved, trying to rise but slumping down again.

"My *back*," he moaned. "My back is broken! That dog has crippled me. . . ."

Louisa burst into tears, covering her face again.

"Where's Bru?" Alec called from the road. "What have they done with Bru?"

Wordlessly Gail pointed toward the woods and saw her father turn and head that way. "Puppy is with him," she called, and Dave nodded as he continued running.

"Go call for an ambulance," Alec said to Gail. He had given Dick a cursory examination, evoking deep, heartfelt groans. "I can't tell anything here. If there is something wrong with his back, and he certainly thinks there is, the worst thing we can do is move him without the proper equipment."

Roger Hewlett's groan was as heartfelt as Dick's. "For heaven's sake, Morgan, there's nothing wrong with the man but fright. All that dog did was knock him down."

"Don't say that," Dick broke in, raising his head weakly. "That dog attacked me, and I'm going to sue."

Gail looked at Alec, nodded and turned toward the house. Better to have proof now that Dick wasn't hurt. As she went she glanced toward the woods. She had seen Dave weaving in and out of the trees, heading south, but she hadn't seen a hint of either Bru or the dog. Her heart hurt for Bru. And for Alec, whose eyes were haunted and sad as he searched the edge of the woods. She looked back as she neared the house and saw that he was still standing with the others but staring off at the trees again.

"I've called an ambulance," Virginia's voice announced, and Gail's head shot up. Her mother was standing in the doorway, looking desperate and harried. "Dave and I saw what happened from the upstairs window, and then Bru came in after the men left and told me Puppy had probably torn off that man's arm, so I thought I'd better call for help."

"Bru came here? *How?*"

"Sneaked in the back way, how else? He had Puppy with him. He's really upset, Gail, he could hardly talk. Listen, isn't that the ambulance?"

"Yes," Gail said helplessly. "Yes, it is. Look—I'd better take Louisa to the hospital in my car, I don't think she's fit to drive, and Mr. Hewlett doesn't drive at all. Please, take special care of Bru. Tell him—tell him Puppy didn't hurt the man and everything is going to be all right. Make him believe it, Mom. I'll tell Alec Bru is here, and he'll go tell Dad to stop searching."

She turned and ran to her station wagon and climbed in, snatching up her samples and estimate sheets, folders, recorder and calculator from the passenger seat and flinging them all in the back. She backed out, wishing she could hold her ears as the ambulance roared around a corner, wailing like a banshee, and came to a stop near Hewlett's Mercedes.

THEY DROVE OFF in a slow procession. More, Gail thought, like a funeral than an emergency trip. The paramedics had done their tests, looked at each other and rolled Dick unceremoniously onto a stretcher. Clearly they thought they didn't need to worry about this one.

"You were right, Doc," one of them said in an aside to Alec. "Only bruised. We'll take him in anyhow and insist on X rays so you've got a record. He sounds like he wants to go to court."

By now Louisa had settled into Gail's wagon gratefully and was chattering away like one of the family. "It's so very nice of you to drive me to the hospital," she said effusively. "It scares me to death to drive that Mercedes of Roger's. He has a fit over every little scratch. What will he do, by the way? Wait there?"

"Alec will take him to my parents' house. He'll be all right."

"Oh, I wasn't worried about him. Heaven knows, Roger can take care of himself. Now Dick is another story. He looks so big and strong, but he's just like a child. Poor darling, he was trying so hard to prove to Roger that he could handle Bruce, but now I suppose that dog has ruined that."

Gail pulled out on the highway behind the ambulance. "I think that Mr. Hewlett had already planned for Mrs. Hewlett to take over the, uh, handling of Bru."

Louisa's mouth drooped. "Oh, dear. Marian's going to be miserable if he starts that. Of course she's very fond of Bruce, but she simply hasn't time to look after a child. Actually, I think she should let Alec have him, but she has reasons for keeping him up north."

Gail stared at her thoughtfully; then, slowing and stopping at a red light, she twisted in her seat. Under the pretext of arranging her scattered materials so they wouldn't fall from the back seat, she touched her recorder. Facing forward again, she felt a slow, hot flush rising in her cheeks. What she was doing was wrong. But what had Alec said? Anything short of murder. This, she reminded herself, was short of murder.

Trying to sound friendly, she said, "I suppose Marian has a great many social duties."

"Exactly," Louisa confirmed as they drove on. "I'm so glad you understand. She's on the go from morning until night. I can't see how Roger could expect her to take care of a nine-year-old boy. That's what servants are for." She hesitated, staring ahead. "I can't see the ambulance, Gail. We lost it waiting at that light."

"It's all right. I know where the hospital is."

"Of course, I should have realized that." Louisa laughed a little and settled back. "I'm not truly worried about Dick, anyway. I'm sure he's not hurt. He's such a baby. If he stubs his toe you'd think his leg was broken. I remember one time—"

"Louisa," Gail interrupted hastily. "I've thought of a marvelous solution for everyone involved in this—this silly quarrel over Bru."

"Really?" Louisa sat up and looked at her brightly. "What?"

Gail could see the top story of the hospital ahead on the next block. So little time. She stumbled over words but got them out. Casually.

"Why not just switch custody times? Send Bru down here to his father during the school year, when there's so much social life going on up north. Then, in the nice lazy days of summer, Bru could visit his mother for, uh, for a little vacation."

"But of course! Marian would love that," Louisa said. "It would be ideal for everyone. In fact, she's often said exactly the same thing herself. But she can't let him go really. He's her spending money."

Pulling in and stopping in the hospital's parking lot, Gail looked confused. "What? I don't understand."

Louisa sighed. "That's because you don't know pinch-penny Roger. He won't give poor Marian any money, only credit cards. He wants to know every little thing she buys, and he's fussy about it. So the only money she can spend as she likes comes from the boy's support payments."

Gail shut off the engine and stared at her. "But she'd have to use that money for Bru, wouldn't she?"

"Lord, no." Gathering up her gloves and purse and opening the door, Louisa giggled. "Roger pays his expenses, gives him an allowance and doesn't mind a bit. He likes Bruce. Anyway, I don't think the old man even knows Alec sends support. Come on, let's go see what's happening to Dick."

Grabbing her coat from the back seat, Gail turned off the recorder, gathered it up with the rest of her materials and tucked it behind the back seat. Then she followed Louisa toward the hospital and the double doors marked Emergency, feeling a bit guilty again. Turning on that device had been a sudden impulse to record and keep anything that might help Alec in his arguments. And maybe she had. But she didn't much like herself for having used the method. She knew very well that Louisa wouldn't have said a word about Marian if she'd known the recorder was on.

"SLIGHT ABRASIONS on his face," the intern said, writing industriously. "From his fall, I suppose. Bruises, such as those caused by blows, on his back. No broken bones, sprains or wounds." He looked up from his report and smiled at Louisa. "You're his wife? He can leave now. Use the side door, please. Don't block the entrance."

Across the waiting room Gail stood up and stretched, looking through the window at the fast-falling darkness. It had taken over two hours to do the testing and X rays Dick had demanded, and it would soon be night. She waited, watching as an aide propelled Dick in a wheelchair toward the side door; then she fell in behind with Louisa and followed.

Once outside, Dick gave up his pretense of great pain and his seat in the wheelchair at the same time. "I've been had," he grumbled as he climbed into Gail's station wagon. "I never had a chance. I should have known those interns and technicians would all be on Morgan's side. That's the medical profession for you. They'd never testify against a doctor."

"The dog is mine," Gail said stiffly. "If you're going to sue, you'll have to sue me. However, I'm not rich."

A dead silence prevailed on the way back to the house. Night had fallen by the time they'd arrived, and the multicolored lights twinkled in the trees again. In the glow they could see that someone had brought up the black Mercedes and parked it in the driveway. Dick looked sourly relieved going in, as if he felt his ordeal were over. But there was no one at the door, no sound of conversation, and suddenly Gail called out, frightened.

"Mom? Where is everybody?"

Virginia appeared immediately at the living room door, with Roger Hewlett behind her. "Oh, Gail! Thank heaven, you're home. Bru . . ." She caught her breath, steadying her voice. "Bru ran away again. He was gone, dog, suitcase and all, when I came back into the house. Dave and Alec are out looking for him."

"That's a trick, Roger," Sommers said, stepping forward. "A very common trick in these cases. They are trying to prevent us from taking the boy back to his mother."

"We certainly are not," Virginia said, bristling. "What right do you have to question what I say?"

"A very good right," Dick said, straightening and staring at her arrogantly. "I'm Marian's brother-in-law and I'm also a lawyer."

"How awful for you," Virginia said with heavy sarcasm. "But we all have our troubles. Try to rise above it."

Sommers reddened. "Now see here. I won't be insulted."

"Shut up, Dick," Hewlett said calmly. "She's right. Bruce did run away and it's mostly your fault. If you hadn't started chasing him none of this—"

"It's not Dick's fault," Louisa said wildly. "He was only trying to show you he could handle Bruce. And anyway, it's foolish to take the boy back to Marian if you're going to make her take care of him. She won't like that, Roger. She—"

"That's enough," Roger said irritably. "Just be quiet."

"Let her talk," Virginia said suddenly. "She's making sense." She smiled at Louisa, who smiled back. "Go ahead," Virginia said encouragingly. "You were saying that Bru's mother wouldn't like..."

"...to take care of him," Louisa finished, nodding. "She's quite fond of him really, but she doesn't like to spend a lot of time around children. They bother her terribly."

Virginia snorted. "Then she shouldn't have had one."

Louisa's eyes widened. "But how could she have known they bothered her if she hadn't had one?"

"Actually," Dick said to Hewlett, "you really should reconsider the case, Roger. Marian definitely wants Louisa and me to take over the responsibility of that child, and if you want your wife to be happy you'll—"

"Enough," Hewlett roared, losing his temper. "Don't be a blind fool. Marian must want to keep her son close to her and care for him herself. Why else would she insist that we bring him back home?"

"Money," Gail said abruptly, amazing herself. She turned red as Hewlett swung around, his mouth open. "It's true," she said, not looking at Louisa. "You don't give her any spending money, and she uses Bru's support payments, instead."

"That's rude, Gail," Virginia admonished, looking critical. "You shouldn't have said that. The financial arrangements between Mr. and Mrs. Hewlett are none of your business."

"There aren't any support payments for Bruce," Hewlett said slowly, frowning at Gail. "I told Marian to stop them when we married. Certainly she would have obeyed . . ." His voice trailed off uncertainly. "You don't think I'm right, do you?" he added in a moment. "Why?"

She could tell him what Louisa had told her; she could go get the recorder and prove it. She could, but she couldn't.

"Because," she began hesitantly, then felt words rising inside like a flood. "Because if Bru's mother were truly loving and caring, he'd want to go back. I don't say she doesn't care for him, but I do say she doesn't care enough. If she did, you couldn't keep him away." She stopped, amazed again, listening to the echo of the words. *It was true for everyone. Real love was a magnet.*

Splotches of red appeared on Roger's pale, harsh-featured face. "You're free with your opinions, Mrs. Sheridan, but I think you're prejudiced. You're in love with Morgan."

"No, she isn't," Virginia said hotly. "He keeps asking her to marry him and she won't even listen."

"Mother!"

Virginia raised her chin. "It's true, isn't it?"

"No," Gail said recklessly. "I do love him. And I am going to marry him. And we're going to keep trying until we get custody of Bru. And we'll do it. We have to. Nine years old is too young to have to cope with loneliness."

"You haven't a chance," Dick said scornfully. "You'll never beat Roger Hewlett in court."

"Shut up, Dick," Roger said flatly. "I can do my own bragging when I think it's necessary." He crossed the hall to the coat rack and took down his muffler and topcoat. "I trust—" he looked back at Dick sardonically "—that you're strong enough to drive as far as a good motel. Come along, Louisa. We'll see you midmorning tomorrow, Mrs. Sheridan. Please have the boy ready. I'm sure you'll find him long before that."

Stubbornly silent, Gail watched them troop out. She stood with equally silent Virginia and listened until the quiet tick of the Mercedes receded in the distance, then spoke.

"Sandwiches, Mom, a thermos of coffee and a flashlight. I'll get a blanket upstairs. I'm going to help Alec and Dad. I have an idea where Bru might have gone."

Ten minutes later Dave walked in alone, looking exhausted, as Gail came down the stairs, carrying the blanket. "Good," he said, glancing at the blanket. "It's getting colder out there. I came back for another light. Ours burned out."

"Where's Alec?"

"Heading south, checking the woods."

"I'll take the car. We'll find Bru, Dad. You stay here. If Bru saw Hewlett and the Sommers leaving, he may come in. If he does, come find us." Shrugging into her coat, she took the sandwiches and coffee from Virginia, grabbed up the blanket and ran out. She was almost sure now that she knew where Bru had gone.

Still, she drove slowly, watching the sides of the road, hoping to see a slim boy with bronze hair, heading home. A mile and a half and there was the black bulk of Alec's unfinished house, the dark gleam of the little lake. The home that was part of Bru's dream.

Catching her breath, Gail turned and bumped up the rutted service road toward the house, pulling to a stop close to a pile of lumber. There were dozens of places a nine-year-old could crawl into and hide. Bru knew that.

The blanket on one arm, flashlight in hand, she made her way up the uneven road toward the house. Suddenly, out of the dark, something large lunged toward her, panting and jingling, pressing against her legs.

"Puppy!" She could have hugged him. "Come on, friend! Take me to Bru!"

He dashed off, too quick for her flashlight beam to catch, and she followed the jingle of his collar. The light flashed back and forth as she tried to see where he'd gone. There. A glimmer of black, leaping into the house. She was almost running now, stumbling over debris.

"Bru!" she called, her voice quavering and high. "Bru! It's Gail! Where are you?"

"I've got him, Gail," came Alec's deep voice, gravelly with fatigue. "He's fine. We just don't have a light. Be careful, there's a lot of trash on the floors."

"Okay. I will." Tears of relief blurred her eyes and she stopped to wipe them. The Dobie brushed against her legs and left again, feet pattering on the rough floor. "Which way?"

"Over here. To the west, angel."

She swept the flashlight beam in an arc, stopping abruptly as the light caught them. Alec was sitting on the floor, leaning against the west wall, Bru was curled in the crook of his arm and Puppy sat beside Bru, panting, showing his white-toothed grin. She rushed to them and knelt, shaking out the blanket and wrapping it around them.

"You look awful," she said crossly. "And you're cold! Why are you just sitting here? The car is warm and I've got coffee and sandwiches. Are you hurt, Alec? Can't you walk?"

"Shh," Alec said, and touched her face gently. "I'm not hurt, only tired. We just found each other a few minutes ago. And we've been talking."

"About next summer, when I get to come back. Dad said you and he tried really hard to have me stay now, but it didn't work out." Bru cleared his throat. "But it's okay, Gail. It'll be great when I finally get to stay."

"Good." She pushed Puppy aside and put her arms around Bru, blanket and all, and hugged him. he hugged her back, hard.

"That's settled then," she said. "We're all going to be waiting for you when school is out. Your dad and me, and Grandpa and Grandma, and Pu—Slash. We'll have a wonderful summer." She felt Alec's gaze on her and looked up. Even in the light of the torch she could see the warmth and wonder in his eyes.

"The best summer," Bru said with conviction. "The best I ever had. I can hardly wait." He pushed back the blanket and scrambled to his feet. "I'm hungry. Can I have one of your sandwiches?"

16

IN TIME everyone calmed down. Starting upstairs, Bru stopped and looked at Dave. "My bike, Grandpa?"

"I got it. It's in my shop. I'll oil it once in a while."

"Thank you."

"You're welcome."

Dave watched him go up the rest of the stairs and turned to Alec. "You can have the couch again if you want to stay, Alec."

"Thanks, Dave, but I'll sleep at home and come back early, if you don't mind. I'm sorry this all came up while Bru was still visiting you. It's a hell of a bother, I know."

Dave smiled. "Bru isn't. They are. I may sic Puppy on that Summers fellow again tomorrow. Sure you want to go home?"

"Yep. I'll tell the ladies good-night." He turned and walked through the dining room into the kitchen, where Gail and Virginia were cleaning up after a late supper. He stood in the doorway, watching Gail moving around and thinking she looked almost too slender. Too pale, too, though her ivory skin still had its touch of rose and her red hair shone beneath the lights. He sighed, feeling old and tired, bitter with his load of disappointment.

"I came to say good-night," he said. "And to thank you. I'll be back in the morning early enough to—to take the problem off your hands."

Gail tossed the dishcloth she held onto the counter-top, and untied the apron she wore. "I'll walk out with you," she said, and met his brooding gaze, her own eyes as serene as a calm summer sky.

Curious, Alec took her arm and went toward the front door. She had looked at him like that before; he remembered it well. That was the day he'd told her he needed her and asked her never to leave him, and she had said she wouldn't. The day he had bought the land for the house. The day their future had seemed so clear to him. Before all their troubles had begun. Going out-side, breathing the sharp, cold air, he wondered if he could be imagining that look just because he wanted so badly to see it again. He stopped at the side of his car and looked down at her, but her gaze was now on the twinkling colors of the Christmas lights.

"Gail?"

She looked up at him inquiringly, but the colored lights reflected and danced in her eyes, and he couldn't read her thoughts.

"You told Bru," he said slowly, "that all of us would be waiting for him next summer."

Gail smiled faintly. She knew the question he was asking in a roundabout way. And after all, she'd walked out here with him to settle it. She shivered a little from the chill in the air and moved closer, sliding her arms around his waist beneath his coat, feeling his arms take her in against his warmth. "We will be," she said with certainty. "You can bring me that silly agreement to-morrow and I'll take it to the lawyer or whatever I have to do. I'm going to marry you."

Alec tightened his arms around her and bent to take her mouth in the gentlest of kisses. "Gail," he mur-mured, his voice uneven, "my angel. I was afraid all this trouble would drive you away from me forever. What changed your mind?"

"Something simple," she said, suddenly smiling. "So simple I felt foolish for not seeing it before. Simple enough that you'll figure it out for yourself someday. For now, just bring me the paper."

Alec laughed, swinging her around. "A puzzle, is it? Who cares what makes a miracle happen as long as it happens? Do you know how happy you've made me?"

"It's only the beginning, darling. We're a family now."

THE MORNING was clear and cold, the sky a bright blue, the sunlight a pale yellow warmth that slowly melted the frost on the shrubs and grass. In the warm kitchen Virginia banged pots and skillet with unnecessary vigor, watching through the window as Bru rode back and forth on his bike. Occasionally she wiped her eyes with the corner of her apron and muttered to herself about the origins and habits of the Hewletts.

"For a gently reared woman, you have a very colorful vocabulary," Gail said.

Virginia looked pained. "Not colorful enough for the occasion. I'll swear, I don't know how I'll get through this day. How can that old man be so cruel? Surely he must know what his own wife is like."

"I'm not certain of that last," Gail said, pouring a cup of coffee. "A couple of things that came out last night seemed to surprise him." Sitting down with the coffee, she smiled at her mother. "Louisa didn't pull any punches."

Virginia gave a sudden laugh. "Louisa is an innocent. She just tells it the way she sees it. You might doubt her judgment, but no one could doubt her word. She's as open as a child. Do you want breakfast?"

Glancing through the window, Gail shook her head. "No, thanks. That's Alec driving up, and it's almost time for Hewlett to arrive." She put down her cup and started to rise, then sat down again and picked up the cup, smiling ruefully at Virginia's questioning look. "Bru might like some time alone with his father," she explained.

Drifting toward the window, Virginia nodded. "He might. But he won't have much. Hewlett's car just came around the bend." She came back to the table and sat down with Gail, biting her lip. "There's nothing left to do, except say goodbye. Puppy is shut up in the wood-shop, the bags are packed and on the steps, Bru's wearing his heavy sweater and he's got money for a snack." Virginia's face was set in mournful lines; her green eyes were dull. Gail patted her hand.

"We'll have him this summer, Mom. And maybe next year we'll have him for good...." She looked up as Dave came in. "Is it time? Should we go out now?" she asked.

"Hell, I don't know," Dave said, clearly upset. "They're talking. Standing out at Hewlett's car, just talking. We saw Hewlett coming and I went with Bru to put up his bike, and when we came back they were talking. Alec told Bru to sit on the steps and wait." Taking the coffee Virginia poured for him, Dave sat down, frowning. "Do you think Alec would get rough with that old man, Gail?"

"I'm sure he wouldn't. Alec isn't like that."

Virginia got up and peered out the window again. "Alec's called Bru over to the car now," she said, biting her lip again. "Maybe we should go out."

Gail sighed. "He won't leave without telling us goodbye, Mom."

"Well, I certainly hope not. I'd hate to think—" Virginia's voice faltered, then came back in a stifled shriek. "He's not going! Hewlett's car is pulling away and Bru is waving goodbye!"

Galvanized by incredible hope, Gail sprang up and ran for the door, plunged outside and stopped, laughing as she saw Bru leap up and hug his father, drop to the ground and tear off for the wood shop to let Puppy out, yelling "Yahoo! Yahoo! Yahoo-o-o-o!" at the top of his voice.

Pounding up the steps, Alec caught her in his arms and swung her around. "Yahoo," he said, breathless and grinning. "Absolutely yahoo! We've got our boy." He looked at Dave and Virginia, poised at the door. "And you two had as much to do with it as anyone. Thank you. Thank you very much."

"But what *happened*? Tell us!"

"Mother!"

"Shh," Alec said. "She needs to know. We all do. Hewlett called home and talked to Marian, and I guess they settled quite a few things. She'll take Bru for a couple of weeks in the summer, during which time she will devote her full time to him, and the rest of the year he's ours. I asked Hewlett what changed his mind, and he said for one thing he'd faced up to how little time Marian wanted to give a child, but mostly it was because he'd had a close, wonderful family life with parents and grandparents when he was bringing up his sons, and once he knew Gail was going to marry me he couldn't deny Bru the same chance."

"Bless him," Virginia said. "He's an angel in disguise. To think I would have cheerfully beaten him to death only yesterday."

"Virginia!"

"Good Lord," Virginia said, peering up at Dave. "Now she has you doing it. Never mind, here comes Bru. Let's all go in and have an immense brunch. We're starving."

"We'll be there in a few minutes," Alec said, and grasped Gail's arm to hold her back. She looked at him and laughed as the door closed on the rest of them.

"We'd better be. I'm not only starving, I'm freezing."

He unbuttoned his coat and pulled her inside, holding it around her, his eyes meeting hers, his look as warm as sunlight, open, vulnerable, without a trace of bitterness.

"I just wanted to say I love you, angel."

She opened her mouth, but no words came. Turning her head, she closed her eyes and let her cheek rest on his shoulder, feeling wonderfully warm and full of glory. It was one thing to suddenly know he really did love her, and quite another to hear him say it. "I knew that last night," she said finally. "But I wasn't sure you'd ever find it out. Did you bring the contract?"

He rubbed his cheek on her silky hair and smiled. "I burned it. I read it over myself, and I couldn't believe how stupid it sounded. Insulting, even. As if I didn't trust you. No wonder you didn't like it."

"You *burned* it?"

"Sure. We don't need anything like that. What made you think we did?"

She stared up at him, at the teasing amusement in his hazel eyes, and then she laughed, her breath misting in the cold air. "Quite true. That paper would have crumbled with age before we'd managed to stay away from each other."

He kissed her once more, taking his time about it. "I love you," he said again, emotionally. "I trust you with my life. You don't have to sign anything. Just promise me love as long as you live."

Gail smiled. "That's in my contract, darling."

"What contract?"

She laughed again and hugged him. "The one the minister reads where you have to say 'I do.'"

"Oh. Well, I will. I mean, I do. Forever."

Harlequin Temptation dares to be different!

Once in a while, we Temptation editors spot a romance that's truly innovative. To make sure *you* don't miss any one of these outstanding selections, we'll mark them for you.

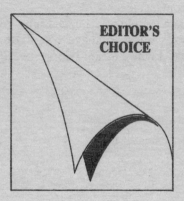

EDITOR'S CHOICE

When the "Editors' Choice" fold-back appears on a Temptation cover, you'll know we've found that extra-special page-turner!

THE

Temptation

EDITORS

You'll flip . . . your pages won't!
Read paperbacks *hands-free* with

Book Mate • I

The perfect "mate" for all your romance paperbacks
Traveling • Vacationing • At Work • In Bed • Studying
• Cooking • Eating

Perfect size for all standard paperbacks, this wonderful invention makes reading a pure pleasure! Ingenious design holds paperback books OPEN and FLAT so even wind can't ruffle pages— leaves your hands free to do other things. Reinforced, wipe-clean vinyl-covered holder flexes to let you turn pages without undoing the strap...supports paperbacks so well, they have the strength of hardcovers!

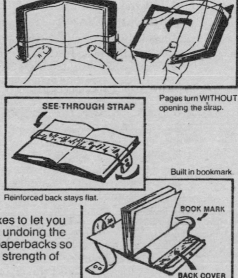

Pages turn WITHOUT opening the strap.

SEE-THROUGH STRAP

Reinforced back stays flat.

Built in bookmark.

BOOK MARK

BACK COVER HOLDING STRIP

10" x 7¼", opened.
Snaps closed for easy carrying, too.

COMING NEXT MONTH

Harlequin Superromance

MORE THAN A FEELING

A powerful new Superromance from

ELAINE K. STIRLING

Andonis Sotera was the kind of man a woman might encounter in a Moroccan café after dark, or on the deck of a luxury cruise ship. In short, Andonis was the kind of man a woman like Karen Miller would never meet.

And yet they fell in love. Suddenly the civil servant from a small Canadian city was swept into the drama of Andonis's life. For he was not only her passionate, caring lover, he was *The Deliverer*, the one man who could save a small Mediterranean country from the terror of a ruthless dictator.

But Andonis needed Karen's help. And she was willing to risk her life to save their love....

MORE THAN A FEELING...
Coming in February from Harlequin Superromance

They went in through the terrace door. The house was dark, most of the servants were down at the circus, and only Nelbert's hired security guards were in sight. It was child's play for Blackheart to move past them, the work of two seconds to go through the solid lock on the terrace door. And then they were creeping through the darkened house, up the long curving stairs, Ferris fully as noiseless as the more experienced Blackheart.

They stopped on the second floor landing. "What if they have guns?" Ferris mouthed silently.

Blackheart shrugged. "Then duck."

"How reassuring," she responded. Footsteps directly above them signaled that the thieves were on the move, and so should they be.

For more romance, suspense and adventure, read Harlequin Intrigue. Two exciting titles each month, available wherever Harlequin Books are sold.